# Love & Liberty

## Holidays in Hallbrook

## Elsie Davis

Sweet Romance Publishing

*Many thanks to all the firefighters in the world who bravely face danger, risking their lives to protect the people and things we love and many thanks to the Audubon Society and all the contributions of bird watchers and organizations around the world who protect our flying friends, and who keep us educated and thirsting for a better understanding of the habitat in which our fine-feathered friends exist.*


*Ecclesiastes 9:11*
*I have seen something else under the sun. The race is not to the swift or the battle to the strong, nor does food come to the wise or wealth to the brilliant or favor to the learned; but time and chance happen to them all.*

Sweet Romance Publishing

Sweetromancepublishing.com

PO Box 778

Liberty, NC 27298

# Chapter One

♥

Ashley Stanton took out two teacups and several kinds of tea in anticipation of her guest's impending arrival. She hadn't seen Tricia, one of her close friends from high school, in almost ten years. Distance and life had a way of tapering off phone calls and well-meaning promises to find a way to get together again. Ashley was more than a little nervous and not sure what to expect. She hadn't planned on coming back to Hallbrook, but then again, divorce hadn't been part of her plan either.

The china looked out of place against the chipped and yellowed counter. Still, there was nothing she could do to make the outdated kitchen look any better than it did. The flowerpot next to the stove was already serving double duty of covering a burn spot and adding a tiny bit of cheer to the otherwise dismal room.

When people returned to their hometown, it was reasonable to want to have something to show for the time away. The tiny cottage she was renting had to be more than a hundred years old, judging by the dingy and cracked kitchen tiles, antiquated appliances, and worn wooden floors in the rest of the house. The rental reflected all she hadn't accomplished over the years, other than some of her own wildlife photography. They were the only thing that brought life to the walls that were in desperate need of a fresh coat of paint.

Luckily, Hallbrook and this cottage were only a stopping point on her journey to start over in life. Ashley hadn't been back here since she left after her mother passed away, the town holding far too many broken-hearted memories. One of the benefits of returning however, was that Trent, her older brother and only other family, would finally meet his nephew face to face.

After that, it was her and Cory against the world. Although, as a four-year-old, he was along for the ride. Unfortunately, until she figured out where she was going to work and live, they'd have to make her limited resources stretch. Child support would only go so far, and her savings account wasn't exactly a picture of wealth.

Her ex-husband had seen to that. If only she'd paid more attention, then she might have seen the divorce coming and would have monitored their accounts more carefully.

Turns out, Joe Stanton was as heartless and selfish as they came. Too bad she hadn't known that when she married him. Instead, she'd been young and naïve and fallen for his good looks, and the attention he showered on her. Life to him was about being a part of the social crowd who flitted from party to party, making deals and contacts. It was all about appearances and a show of wealth. Ashley may have had the title of wife, but in Joe's world, the term meant nothing more than *arm candy*.

"Cory, honey, are you hungry?" She gazed at her son, loving his curly brown hair and blue eyes. He was the spitting image of her, something she'd discovered when she'd gone through her own baby pictures.

"Yes, Mommy. Look, I'm almost finished my drawing for your friend." He held up the picture he'd been working on for the past ten minutes.

"I didn't realize you were drawing the picture for Tricia. That's very sweet of you, honey. And I'm sure Tricia will absolutely love it. What a beautiful horsey," she said, smiling at her son. She overlooked the oversized belly and stick legs and saw the love he'd put into the drawing.

"I'll make you a peanut butter and jelly sandwich. Your favorite. Tricia should be here soon, and while you eat lunch, she and I have will have a chance to chat. Mommy hasn't seen her in almost ten years. We have a lot to catch up on." That was an understatement. The two had been close in high school, but after Ashley's mother died, she'd headed west for California and left the past, and Hallbrook, behind. This wasn't the first time she found herself starting over.

"Ten years is a long time. That's more years than I am, 'cause I'm only four."

"You're right. That's an excellent point." Cory was the light of her life and kept her extremely busy. He was also the reason she was determined to move forward after the divorce and find a way to fix the mess she'd made of her life.

The call from the National Audubon Society had come as a surprise, but even more so once they explained the reported sighting was in the Hallbrook area of the White Mountain National Forest. Her hometown. And precisely the reason the New Hampshire branch of the Audubon Society wanted her to join the Bald Eagle Project. It had given her a sense of renewed hope and faith in the future, that things were looking up. A positive sign to lead her back to the east coast. It had also given her something to focus on other than Joe and his betrayal.

Cory picked up another crayon, returning his focus to the drawing. Ashley went into the kitchen and made him a sandwich. She poured him a glass of milk, grabbed a napkin, and delivered lunch to her budding artist. She'd been blessed with a sweet child that rarely gave her trouble. Pure of heart, he was a joy to all who met him.

There was a knock at the door, and Ashley took a deep breath, trying to calm her nerves. What did one say to an old friend you'd been close to, but then ditched? When Ashley had called Tricia, her friend's enthusiasm had prompted the invitation. It would be nice to have someone in town to talk to other than Trent. Especially, since he was currently out of town on a business trip.

The last thing Ashley wanted was for people in Hallbrook to know the dirty details of her personal life. She'd learned the hard way it was better to keep her distance from people, that way, they couldn't hurt her. Better just to say she was divorced and act happy about it. People would ask fewer questions, ones she didn't want to answer.

Ashley pulled open the door. Tricia hadn't changed much over the years, and she would have recognized her anywhere. "I'm so glad you could come over," she said, stepping forward to give Tricia a warm embrace, hoping to ease through the awkward first few minutes.

"Are you kidding? I wouldn't miss coming to see you. I couldn't believe my ears when you called and told me you were coming back to Hallbrook. I wish I could've met up with you last week when you arrived and given you a proper welcome. But between work, Harry, and the kids, I've been swamped. And with his relatives in town for the annual July 4$^{\text{th}}$

reunion, my place is a madhouse." Tricia's bubbly non-stop response reminded Ashley of old times. Her friend was still a happy-go-lucky person who embraced life with all its challenges, and even managed to smile.

"Today's a good day for a visit. I just finished unpacking the last of the boxes. Not that I brought much with me. I'm traveling light, or as light as one can with a young son." Ashley rolled her eyes, knowing Tricia would understand since she had two kids of her own. "I can't wait to meet your family."

She led Tricia toward the kitchen table. "This is Cory, my son. He's four, going on ten."

"I've got one of those." Tricia grinned. "Hi, Cory. Aren't you a cutie?" Her friend ruffled Cory's hair, something most people couldn't resist because of the curls.

"Hi, Miss Tricia. I'm making you a picture." He held up the drawing, and Ashley prayed her friend would understand the importance. Cory was friendly with people, but Ashley was worried about him making new connections since they'd had to leave behind everyone he knew in California.

"*Awww.* I love it. What a great horse picture. It's very kind of you to do this for me. I'll be sure to hang it on my refrigerator. Thank you."

"You're welcome." Cory's eyes twinkled with pleasure under the heavy praise.

"And I love your manners. You need to come and play with my kids and teach them a thing or two."

Ashley's heart swelled with pride. Cory was a great kid, and she wouldn't let Joe's rejection influence her son's approach to life and people. That final day in the courthouse, Ashley had vowed to never trust anyone again and give them the power to hurt her or Cory. And it was a vow she intended to keep.

"It looks like the horse is eating peanut butter and jelly for lunch, too." Tricia grinned, but Cory was lost, his face scrunched up in confusion. "You've got peanut butter and jelly all over your face. And look, I can see some, right there," she said by way of explanation and pointed at the horse's head.

Cory giggled. "Guess he did."

Sometimes, kids were the best ice breaker. Ashley was already feeling more relaxed. "Can I fix you a cup of tea?"

"That sounds great. I need to unwind and breathe after the circus at my house." Tricia followed her into the kitchen. Ashley didn't miss her friend's quick glance around and was grateful when she didn't comment. Tomorrow, she'd change out the putrid curtains that looked as old as the cottage.

Ashley plugged in the electric tea kettle and switched it on high. "What kind would you like? I've got chamomile, vanilla chai, and orange cinnamon and, of course, plain black pekoe." She pointed at the boxes, taking out an orange cinnamon teabag for herself.

"I'll have what you're having. Orange cinnamon sounds delicious."

"It's my favorite. We can wait in the living room for it to heat." They moved into the other room and sat across from each other. The house came furnished, and Ashley was embarrassed by the threadbare sofa and scratched coffee table. Judging by the gnawed lower sections of all four legs, a dog had turned the table into his own personal dinner once upon a time. Ashley looked forward to when she could afford her own furniture again.

"So, tell me what's going on with you? I'm dying to hear what brought you back to Hallbrook after all these years? And where's that husband of yours? Did he come with you?" Tricia had no problem jumping right in to find out the reason for the sudden return to town.

Ashley looked out the front window, past the faded-blue drapes. This is the part where the conversation got tough. She took a deep breath, willing herself to be strong. There was no reason for anyone to know the truth. To know that Joe had walked out on her, moving on to be with a younger woman. A childless younger woman, to be exact, as he'd pointed out repeatedly.

Too late she realized he'd been serious about not wanting children. The one time they discussed it, she'd been sure he was joking. After all, w*ho didn't want kids*? And when Cory came along by accident, Ashley found out how serious Joe had been. To him, children represented the end of his freedom.

"Joe and I are divorced." There's not much to tell, but trust me, it's a good thing. Cory and I are excited to be back in Hallbrook, even if it's only temporary. I want to show my son where I grew up."

Direct and to the point but glossing over the ugly details. For years, she prayed Joe would grow to love his son, but it never happened. Instead, he'd spent that time with another woman and had been systematically draining their accounts in preparation of his new life. One that didn't include her or their son.

"What brings you back to Hallbrook? What to do you plan to do?" Tricia asked with genuine interest.

"As a wildlife photographer, I can take my work anywhere. When I got a call from the Audubon Society about a bald eagle being sighted near here, I jumped at the opportunity to investigate. It would be exciting if there is a nest practically in our backyard. If one considers White Mountain National Forest, our backyard." Ashley chuckled.

"That would be awesome if you were the one to find it. Local girl comes home and brings fame and fortune to Hallbrook. I can see the headlines now." Her friend laughed, even though she was taking it a little far. "Beats me running numbers all day trying to balance books for corporate clients. Capital B-O-R-I-N-G."

"I do love my job, but then, being outdoors has been my thing."

"Will you stay in Hallbrook after you're done?"

"Probably not. I've applied for a job in Washington D.C. with the National Geographic Society. I'd love to travel all over the world, taking pictures of animals and landscapes, especially if I can work with the National Geographic Kids publication." It was the job she'd always dreamed of. The time she'd spent in California had taken her away from pursuing it, but now that she was back on the east coast, Ashley was ready to try again.

"What about Cory? Won't that make it difficult to travel?"

"Cory will be five soon, and I thought I could homeschool him. He'd get the educational experience of a lifetime as he travels the world with me." Ashley knew it wouldn't be easy, but if given the opportunity, she'd find a way to make it work. It was that important.

"Sounds like you have it all planned out. How long will you be in Hallbrook then?" Tricia asked.

"I'm not sure. I guess long enough to look for the eagle and wait to see what happens with the National Geographic job opportunity. I've got feelers out in a few other places with a couple of smaller magazines, and even an inquiry at a gallery in Boston. However, that one would be a long shot. The timing was perfect to come back to the east coast, which will make it easier if I get an offer." Ashley shrugged, unsure of a lot of things, including her exit strategy. Searching for the bald eagle was a fantastic opportunity to do something meaningful. Something that would bring a much-needed boost of confidence to her life after Joe had managed to rip several layers away.

"I envy the freedom you have. I mean, I'm sorry about the divorce and all, but you look like you've got it together. Not that I regret any of the choices I made, but still, your life sounds far more exciting than mine."

"Thanks. I'd like to think I have it together anyway." Ashley chuckled. "But there's something to be said for stability. I'm sure you have an amazing husband and kids."

"I do at that." Tricia nodded.

"Mommy," Cory said, the tone of his voice alarming.

Ashley started to rise, concerned about what might be wrong. "What is it, honey? What's wrong?" she asked, advancing toward him.

"*Ummm*, there's a scary fire." He frowned and pointed to the kitchen.

"Fire?" Ashley raced to the kitchen, Cory's words sending her into a panic. Just as she reached the doorway, the smoke alarm began emitting a high-pitched screech. "Oh my gosh, the kitchen is on fire. Tricia, call 911. We've got to get out of the house." The flames were already licking at the ceiling, the fire too big for her to put out. She wasn't even sure if there was a fire extinguisher in the place.

*Whoosh*. The kitchen curtains caught fire and were destroyed in seconds, the old, dry material like gasoline. The acrid odor of smoke burned her nose.

*Cory*. The only thing that mattered was getting him to safety. Ashley scooped her son into her arms, adrenaline racing through her body as she tried to think clearly and not overreact. Cory started to cry. They headed for the door, Ashley clutching him tightly. She stopped only to grab her briefcase and camera bag. Luckily, she'd left them by the front door for tomorrow's expedition into the forest.

Tricia followed her outside. They headed for the sidewalk, well away from the house and close to where her friend had parked.

"I called, and they're on their way. I made sure they knew everyone is out of the house." Tricia's calm attitude despite the danger was exactly what she needed to help her remain focused.

"This is awful. I can't imagine what would've started the fire. Thank goodness Cory said something." Ashley couldn't believe what was happening, but as she heard sirens in the distance coming closer and closer, it was becoming more real than she wanted. It was just one more thing in a long line of failure and setbacks. And what if it was her fault? The only thing she'd done was turn on the tea kettle.

She fought to control her emotions for Cory's sake, hugging him close. "I'm so proud of you for telling me about the fire."

Everything they owned was in the house. *Everything.* What if the fire department couldn't save the cottage? Ashley prayed that wouldn't happen. She took a deep breath and exhaled.

*Everyone was safe.* And that's what was most important. Not things. Just people. *Thank you, Lord.* She drew another cleansing breath and tried to hold on to that thought.

The owners of the rental would be furious, and Ashley prayed they had adequate insurance coverage. Judging by the smoke pouring from the house, if the firefighters didn't arrive soon, they might not ever find out what caused the fire. In the space of minutes, her life had turned into another round of turmoil.

The loud wailing grew closer.

"Are the fire trucks coming here, Mommy?" Cory tried to get down out of her arms.

She set him down but kept firm hold of his hand. "Yes, honey. They'll stop the fire, and everything will be okay."

"They're here." Tricia pointed at the fire trucks as they rounded the corner, sirens blasting. "Maybe we should move off to the side." Her friend took her arm and led her to the farthest point down the sidewalk away from the driveway.

Two fire trucks pulled up, and the firefighters jumped off the enormous red vehicles and went into action. Everywhere she looked, firefighters dressed in long, yellow fireproof jackets and galoshes went to work. Some unloaded the hoses off the trucks. A couple of them disappeared behind the house, while others stayed in front and headed for the front door.

One of the firefighters pushed the door open and smoke came pouring out. The man lowered his oxygen mask into place before entering the cottage. Ashley said a prayer for the man's safety.

A black Dodge truck pulled up, and the lone occupant stepped out of the vehicle with a beautiful dalmatian hot on his heels. Ashley watched as the man assessed the situation and called out directions to some of the firefighters. He turned to look her way and then headed straight toward her.

*David Beckett.* Her brother's best friend. And her ex-boyfriend. The man who'd broken her heart with no reason back in high school.

Of course, it had to be David. With everything else in her life going to pot, Ashley wasn't surprised at another heaping dose of insult to injury being added.

Ashley's hand moved to touch the eagle pendant she'd worn ever since David had given it to her. He'd told her the eagle represented freedom, independence, and his love. He wanted her to follow her dreams and travel the world to discover the beauty of wildlife and nature. It was the one thing from David she hadn't been able to expunge from her life. That, and her memories, of course.

For Ashley, the pendant was a symbol of freedom and independence, not undying love. Because one thing she knew for a certainty, David's love had died.

# Chapter Two

♥

DAVID FROZE FOR A second as he recognized the face of a woman he hadn't seen in over a decade. *Ashley Anderson.* She was married now, and for the life of him, he couldn't remember her new last name, although he was sure her brother had mentioned it. *Selective memory?*

He'd known someone had moved into town and rented the old cottage, but Ashley? That was like a punch to the solar *plexus. Twice.* David hadn't seen her in over eleven years, not since he went away to college with Trent, his best friend, and her brother.

After Ashley's mother passed away and she moved to California, Ashley hadn't come back to Hallbrook to his knowledge. At least Trent had never said anything to him about it. But he knew for sure that since he'd moved back to town a few years ago, she hadn't been around. He'd missed seeing Ashley, but he also realized it was better that way. *Out of sight, out of mind.*

*Or almost.*

*Woof.* David shoved memory lane aside, Kojak forcing him back to the here and now. Which included putting out a fire. That was his only goal and demanded his total attention. Part of his job, however, meant dealing with Ashley. Kojak walked next to him, the dog just as much on the job as he was.

"Ladies," David said, nodding in their general direction. "Our initial report states there are no people or animals inside. Is that still accurate?" He tried to keep his voice level and businesslike.

"Yes." Tricia Hunter spoke up. David remembered she'd been close friends with Ashley in high school, so it was no surprise to see her here.

"Perfect. I needed to double-check just to be sure there are no wires crossed. I'm sure the guys will have the fire contained shortly. Any idea what happened?" David was itching to break away and help the team get the fire under control. Still, the questions were important if they wanted to know what they were dealing with and see any potential problems that might arise. He didn't like surprises.

David addressed them both, but his gaze never left Ashley and the boy she picked up and held clutched to her chest. The kid looked just like her. The son Trent had mentioned almost four years ago. *Cute kid. Just like his mother.*

"I don't know. I plugged in a kettle, and we were just sitting in the living room chatting. The next thing I know, Cory was telling me there was a fire in the house. I raced to the kitchen, but it was too late. The flames were already spreading across the wall and up toward the ceiling. I grabbed Cory, and we got out." Ashley looked distraught. Her jaw was clenched, and there was fear in her eyes as she recounted the story.

David's heart went out to her. He wished he could make her feel better about what she was witnessing, but there was nothing he could say to a person to wipe away the stress of a housefire. It was something everyone feared, but luckily, most never experienced.

And then there was the small matter of their past. He had to keep his distance. When it came to Ashley, he was weak. He'd almost followed in his father's footsteps and fallen in love, wanting to spend the rest of this life with the gorgeous brunette standing in front of him. Trent had come to his rescue, providing him the perfect out to end things before he made a huge mess of his life. *And Ashley's.*

"Have you had any other problems with the place since you moved in? Any issues with the wiring before?" The place was old, which meant the cottage came with its own set of necessary updates to keep the place up to code. Ashley didn't seem to realize it, but her comment about the flames licking up the walls meant something to him. He'd keep his guesses to himself until he had more information, and the investigation was complete.

"No." She shrugged. "I mean, the lights have flickered a couple of times. And a couple of switches don't work, but it's an old house, so I'm not surprised. Do you think my kettle was defective?" Her nervous glance in the direction of the house told him that's exactly what she thought.

"I didn't say that," he said, trying to alleviate her fears. Ashley was always quick to think everything was her fault, like she deserved to be blamed for things. She'd even assumed it was something she'd done when he'd broken it off with her, although nothing could have been further from the truth. That was all on him. "I'm trying to get a sense of what was going on when it happened. I'm the battalion chief of the White Mountain Fire Department, and I need to piece together what might have happened and point the investigators in the right direction if possible."

"I understand. Thanks, David. You've done well for yourself. Battalion chief and all. Taking after your father, I see." Ashley smiled, and the sight caught him off guard. Her smiles were something he hadn't been able to forget. But then he'd never stopped looking at the photo he kept of her in his wallet. For old times' sake.

As to taking after his father, he hoped not. Justin Beckett had loved his wife and son more than anything, but he'd given everything to his job as a firefighter. Including his life. As a kid, David wanted to follow in his dad's footsteps. It was in his blood.

Right? But it was more than that to him now. His father had talked about the day they would serve side by side as a team. But it hadn't worked out that way.

Today, he was a firefighter to honor his father's legacy. "Something like that." It was the closest he'd come to talk about the past.

"Can I pet the doggy, Mr. Fireman?" the little boy asked, struggling to get down.

"It's all right by me, if it's all right by your mother. Kojak is a friendly dog." He looked at Ashley for confirmation.

"That's fine." She set Cory down on the ground, holding one of his hands as he approached the dog.

"Hold out your hand so he can smell you first. Dogs like to recognize new friends by sight and smell," David explained, kneeling next to Kojak. "Easy, boy." He didn't need to say anything, but it never hurt for a newcomer to hear the words to put them at ease.

Cory reached his hand out tentatively, doing as David suggested. Seconds later, Kojak sniffed his hand and then licked it, causing the little boy to laugh. David knew from experience the dog's tongue could be ticklish.

The two of them had been a team for over five years now, ever since David rescued him as a one-year-old. Kojak had become the fire department's mascot and a fantastic fire dog after David put him through the training and served as his partner. David trusted Kojak with his life, which wasn't something he would say about everyone he met.

"Hi, Kojak. My name is Cory. I like you." The little boy looked up at David and smiled. "Why does your doggy have all those black spots?"

"Because he's a dalmatian. Kojak is special because he's a fire dog," David explained.

"What's a fire dog?" Cory was apparently one of those inquisitive boys, but David didn't mind.

"A fire dog is on the scene to help us look for trouble. They can rescue people and alert us to danger. They're trained just like a firefighter to know what to do in certain situations. This is a standard house fire, and with no one inside, so he's helping me keep an eye on things from out here." Other than the minor distraction of meeting Cory, that is.

"I saw a fire dog once in a cartoon. His name was Sparky. I liked Sparky. He was a dalmatian, too," Cory said, beaming with pride that he'd remembered all that information.

"Yes, I've heard of him. He's a very famous fire dog." David clapped the boy on the shoulder. "You have a good memory, young man."

"Thanks." Cory hugged Kojak. Friendly kid with excellent manners. Ashley was a good mother—not that he'd expected otherwise.

"Hey, Chief." Scott, one of the firefighters from the local crew, approached. "The fire's under control. The flames spread quickly through the walls and burnt up the floor. Between the water damage and fire damage, I'm not sure the place is salvageable. I'll know more once the fire's completely out."

"Thanks for the update, Scott."

The man glanced at Ashley and then at Tricia. "Sorry, ladies. Hate to be the bearer of bad news, but whatever's left in there will probably have enough smoke and water damage that you won't want it. It'll be a complete loss."

"Everything?" Ashley's voice broke on the one word.

David didn't know her situation, but anytime someone lost everything, it was never good.

"This is awful. I'm so sorry, Ashley," Tricia wrapped an arm around her shoulder and drew her close.

"Did you have renter's insurance?" David asked, knowing the answer based on her forlorn expression. A lot of renters didn't have it when they needed it most.

"No. I just got here and hadn't even given it any thought." Ashley bit her lower lip, a habit she had when she was emotionally undone. Some things never changed. He just wished he could change the outcome of this situation for her.

"That's unfortunate. Do you have a place to stay?" He didn't want to let her think too much about what was already done. It was better to focus on the what-next rather than dwell on the past.

"I'm sure I'll figure something out," she said, her voice breaking.

Ashley had been his friend before she'd become his girlfriend, not to mention, she was his best friend's sister. Trent would never forgive him if he didn't offer to help. "You could stay with me." He shrugged, trying to play down the significance of his words. If she knew how fast his heart was racing just by asking, she'd more than likely run back to California. "I've got plenty of room."

Ashley stared at him as if he'd grown two heads. Any emotion she'd been wearing on her sleeve vanished with his simple offer to help. The new steely determination in her expression more than proved how she felt about him, even before she spoke. "I don't think so. I may be in a difficult position, but I'm not desperate. I think once around with you was more than enough." Her eyes had grown cold and hard, but it was her words that packed a powerful punch.

"Suit yourself. I've got a perfectly good garage apartment available for use. My mother's recovering in a medical rehab facility after leg and hip surgery. She won't need the place for at least another month." It wouldn't be comfortable having Ashley live there, but it was a far cry better than living in the house with him. That, even he couldn't do. He cared far too much about her. Something else that had never changed.

Ashley looked dumbfounded, narrowing her eyes at him. She let out a deep breath and shook her head. "Thanks, but no thanks. I'm sure I'll figure something out. Trent will put us up on the couch, I'm sure."

Except Trent wasn't in a position to offer her a place to stay. And if his friend had felt strong enough about who dated and didn't date his sister back in high school, imagine what he'd say to her living with two single men. *Young, single men.*

Ashley would find out soon enough when she talked to Trent. That was one conversation he didn't want to have with her. "Let me know if there's anything I can do to help. Once upon a time, we were friends, and I'd like to think of us as friends still. And friends help friends. If for no other reason, let me help for Trent's sake."

"Thanks for the generous offer, but I'm sure I can work things out on my own." Ashley took her son by the hand and drew him close.

Tricia, on the other hand, didn't look so sure as she gazed back and forth between the two of them, the questioning look on her face all too clear.

# Chapter Three

♥

STAYING WITH DAVID WOULD be like taking a step back in time. Moving backward. And that was something Ashley was determined not to do. Once around the block with David had been enough to leave a lasting hurt. And after her marriage ending the way it did, she wasn't willing to fall into the trap of love again. *Not with anyone, and especially not with David.*

She'd been shocked by his offer to stay at his place. Outraged was more like it. He was the one who had broken things off with her. The one who'd walked away. When he'd calmly suggested he could waltz back in her life, and she could just move in with him, it had sent her over the edge.

How was she to know he hadn't been talking about moving into his house with him? But it was too late to take back the response she'd fired off before she knew all the facts. His offer of the garage apartment and his pointed remark about the reasons he would extend the offer were obvious.

He wasn't interested in her. He was interested in doing the right thing. Good old, David. Nice guy extraordinaire. Or so she once believed.

David headed for his truck, Kojak following close on his heels.

"Bye-bye, doggy." Cory waved at the dog, his pout making it clear he wasn't happy they were leaving. Ashley and her son were on polar-opposite sides regarding their departure.

"I see things between the two of you haven't changed," Tricia said, shaking her head, a broad grin on her face. Her friend was way off base.

"What do you mean?" Ashley frowned. She didn't have time to discuss David or the past, but the question slipped out before she could stop it. What she really needed to do was find a place to stay tonight and for the next few weeks she was in town.

"Sparks fly when the two of you get together. Always did, and apparently, always will."

"Combustible sparks, maybe. The kind that starts fires and burns everything in their path," Ashley mumbled.

"Then it's a good thing David is a firefighter." Tricia winked.

Ashley wasn't amused. "I've got to find us a place to stay." It wasn't as though her savings account was brimming over with excess funds, and she preferred not to drain what she had on a hotel. Luckily, Trent was just a phone call away.

"I wish I could offer you and Cory a room at my place or even the couch, but with Harry's family in town for the holiday, I'm already overrun. I'm so sorry," Tricia's tone was more than sincere.

"Don't worry about it. It's not your fault. I'll just call Trent and see what he can do to help me. He's not due back into town until next week, but he must have a spare key somewhere. Cory and I should be able to crash at his place. No big deal." Except when she'd first mentioned to Trent that she was coming to town; he hadn't offered for her to stay at his place. Which, at the time, Ashley found odd. Not that she would have agreed. They'd fought enough while growing up over his sloppy living habits and inability to clean up a kitchen. The guy could dirty every dish in the house, but clean one? Never.

"Okay. I'll let you make that call. I'm sorry our reunion wasn't what we were hoping for, but hopefully, when things calm down, we can do this again. What can I do to help in the meantime?"

"Don't worry about it. I'll handle the situation, just like I always do. Cory and I will be fine." Brave words for a woman who currently only owned the clothes on her back, her car, and had no place to stay.

"I can get you some clothes. We're about the same size. And I'm sure I've got something that will fit Cory from the massive amounts of kid's clothes I possess. And why don't you bring Cory to the house to play with Chloe, Bryan, and the others whenever you're out searching for the eagle. I can at least make your life easier that way."

"That's a sweet offer, but I don't want to impose. I'm sure I can figure something out, and Cory will be all right with me."

Tricia shook her head. "It's not an imposition. Trust me. After a day or two out hiking in the woods with you, he won't be so happy. Please, it will help keep the peace in my house. More kids, less fight time, because they can break into happy little groups. Trust me, I know."

It was an ideal offer and certainly better for Cory. "Okay, if you're sure. It would be a big help. And I promise to keep the days short."

"That sounds perfect. I'm glad you're back in Hallbrook, even if it's temporary. I just hate this—" she gestured toward the house, "—was part of your welcome."

"Brings new meaning to the expression coming in a blaze of glory," Ashley said, aiming for humor but landing closer to sarcasm.

"You always were the strong one. I'll let you call Trent and I should probably run. Let me know if you change your mind, and please, don't hesitate to call me for anything."

Strong outwardly, perhaps. Inwardly, not so much. But that was a part of herself Ashley refused to show the world. It wasn't like it would do any good, and she had to keep a brave face for Cory. Everything was about her son.

"Thanks, Tricia. We'll be fine." Ashley hugged her friend, grateful for her strength and offer to help.

"Bye, Cory." Tricia leaned down to hug him.

"Bye, Miss Tricia. I'm sorry about your picture. It's probably all burned up in the fire. I'll make you another one, I promise." Cory was so strong and brave about everything that was happening, and it made Ashley more determined to do the same.

"I look forward to it, Cory. Maybe this time, the horsey could be eating broccoli." She chucked him under the chin.

"*Ummm,* no. My horsey doesn't like broccoli." *More like Cory didn't like broccoli.* Ashley smiled. Even with everything going on, her son had the power to make her forget and treasure the special things in life.

Tricia laughed. "See you tomorrow, Cory." She lifted her hand in farewell as she headed for her car.

Ashley watched her friend as she drove away, not wanting to see the house, or David, for that matter. She dialed Trent's number, relieved when he answered on the first ring. "Hey, Trent. It's Ashley."

"Hey, sis. Are you all settled in? I hate that I wasn't in town when you arrived." Trent may be a terrible housemate, but he was a full-out big brother, complete with a fortified protective mode that put Sir Galahad to shame.

When she'd split with Joe, it had been all she could do to keep him from coming to California and confronting her ex. *Code for kick his butt.* It's why she didn't tell Trent the whole truth, and never would. It was better for everyone this way. "Actually, no. That's why I'm calling."

"What's wrong?" Trent's voice was instantly filled with concern. "Do you need me to cancel this business trip and come home?" Trent would move mountains to make sure she was okay, but he couldn't protect her from life. Something he'd never understood, but something she loved about him. After their mother passed away, Hallbrook had too many painful memories, and she'd hightailed it out of there, much to Trent's consternation.

"No, no, nothing like that. But before I tell you what happened, just know that Cory and I are fine." She knew he'd go ballistic, so it was better to get the most essential information out there first. If only to keep him calm.

"Now you're making me nervous," Trent said, tension evident in his voice.

"The place I rented caught fire. It's a total loss."

"Seriously? Thank God, you're okay. What happened?"

It was one thing to be brave in front of David and Tricia, but Trent knew her better than anyone. Her guard slipped a little, the act of saying the words out loud wringing out emotions she'd been trying to keep on lockdown. Ashley glanced down at Cory, watching her son's fascination with the firefighters in action. The adoration she saw in his eyes was not a sentiment she echoed, or at least not for one firefighter in particular. "Totally serious. I don't know what happened. Trent, I'm worried it was my electric kettle, and that the fire is my fault. I'm not sure what that means to me. I can't afford to replace the house." Ashley voiced the fear that continued to grow.

"Stop worrying. Let the investigators do their job, and let God carry your worries. He's got strong shoulders." Trent's words took her by surprise.

Not that Ashley minded, but in the past, her brother had been resistant to any of her attempts to share her spirituality with him. "Since when did you start handing out biblical messages?"

"Since I've been reading the chronological order version of the Bible, and everything is falling into place. It was the best Christmas gift you could have given me."

"I'm happy to hear it." Ashley smiled. Good things were revealed during hard times, one just had to look harder to see them. "Listen, I'm in a bit of a bind. The house isn't livable right now and might not be again. One of the firefighters mentioned condemning the place. I need somewhere to stay. I, um, can't really afford a hotel right now with all the changes going on in my life." It was as close as she'd come to admitting she was broke. "I was hoping maybe you left a key, and we can stay at your place for a bit. I promise, Cory and I won't get in the way. He's a good kid, and it'll just be until I can find another place."

"Stop. I love Cory, and you know it. Normally, it wouldn't be a problem. I would've insisted you both stay with me if I had space, but I don't."

"What do you mean? Did Maria move in with you? Isn't that risky to have the judge's daughter move in without the benefit of a ring on her finger? The judge has always been pretty old-school if I remember right." Ashley shook her head, both for her brother's short-sightedness as well as for the realization he wasn't willing to put her up—not even for a little while.

"*Whoa.* Wrong track, little sister. The judge *is* old-school, and Maria and I aren't living together. I'm not crazy. I took in a couple of roommates, and a bachelor pad isn't exactly conducive to having you or Cory around, if you know what I mean?"

"Wow. I didn't see that coming." It explained everything, and she had to agree with Trent that it didn't sound like a good match for her and Cory. But it didn't help her situation one iota.

"Sorry, sis. There must be someone else you can call."

*Not anyone she would trust.* Ten years was a long time. Not to mention, people in this town could be nosy and would ask questions. And as far as Ashley was concerned, her private life was off-limits, and she intended to keep it that way. "Don't worry, I'll figure something out."

She spun around and faced the house, and her gaze landed on David. He was headed for his truck, Kojak right beside him.

*Find someone I trust.* Once upon a time, she'd trusted David with everything. And in return, he'd broken her heart. Maybe, just maybe, she should trust him again. But this time, trust him with every-thing *except* her heart. This time, she'd go in knowing full well what to expect. That is, if his offer of the garage apartment was still an option considering her initial response.

"I think I know where I can go. I'll see you next week when you get into town." Ashley nodded, gaining confidence in her decision.

"What do you have in mind?" Trent asked.

"David Beckett. He's one of the firefighters who showed up with the fire department. He offered me a place to stay."

"David's a good guy, but you just got back into town, Ashley. I don't think living with him is the right way to go," Trent's voice bristled, his displeasure obvious. Her brother failed to realize she was grown up and capable of making her own choices.

"Not living with him. Living in his garage apartment." He'd jumped to the same conclusion she had. That made her feel a little better.

"That would be okay then, I guess."

"You guess?" Ashley asked, the word giving her pause. You either trust him or you don't."

"As long as you don't fall in love with him. I know how hurt you were the last time, and I'd hate to see it happen again. Things were pretty rough for a while." She didn't need the reminder. There'd been no explanation from David. No reason. Just a cold-hearted decision to end things between them.

"What do you know about that?" Eleven years was a long time to still be wondering what had gone wrong, but it didn't change the fact that she did.

"Nothing." Trent's crisp response didn't sound like nothing. "I just knew you were moping around for months."

"You have nothing to worry about. I can barely tolerate the man, so I think my heart is safe." Barely tolerate, yes. Although deep down, the ache associated with being near the only man she'd ever really loved caused her heart far too much pain.

"Good. Keep it that way." Trent's words were confirmation of what she already knew. David needed to remain off her radar when it came to matters of the heart. Obviously, Trent knew his friend well enough to know he hadn't changed.

David opened the truck door, and Kojak jumped inside. David climbed in after him and settled in the driver's seat.

"I've got to run. I'll text you later and let you know where I land." Ashley hung up and slid the phone in her pocket. She lifted Cory in her arms and headed for the truck. "*Ummm*, David, can I talk to you for a second?"

"Sure thing. Stay, Kojak," he instructed the dog, before sliding back out of the front seat and coming to stand next to her. "What's up?" he asked, the firm set of his jaw not overly friendly or encouraging.

Ashley looked down at the ground. "I talked to Tricia, and she doesn't have any room. I talked to Trent, and apparently he has roommates."

"I knew that, but I figured you'd find out soon enough." She looked up in time to catch David's shrug, as if it mattered little to him one way or the other.

Ashley's chin rose a notch in defiance. She set a squiggling Cory down, keeping a firm hold of his hand. His preoccupation with the firefighters was a good thing considering he wasn't paying much attention to the grownups or what they had to say. "You could've said something."

"You made it clear what you think of me. I'm not sure you would have welcomed anything I had to say or believed me for that matter."

"Well, once upon a time, I believed in you, but as I recall, you're the one who changed that." This wasn't the way she intended the conversation to go. Bringing up the past would only make everything harder between them.

"Ashley, let it go. That was a long time ago and a lot has happened since then. You're married and have a child. I'd say things worked out pretty well for you." David glared, challenging her to contradict him.

He was right. The way her life had turned out hadn't been his doing. "I'm divorced." Now, why had she gone and told him that when it didn't sound as if Trent had said a word?

David's eyes widened a notch, shock crystal clear in them. "I'm sorry, I didn't know."

"It's all good." She nodded, pasting a smile on her face. False bravado was better than plain cowardice. "It was my choice to come back to Hallbrook."

"I see. Well, I guess that's a good thing."

"Yes. It is. Listen, earlier was more of a knee-jerk reaction than a well-thought-out answer." It was the closest she would come to an apology to him. "You mentioned a garage apartment. If the offer is still open, I'd like to take you up on it. I can pay you the same amount I was paying to rent this place."

"The offer is still open, but no payment is necessary. My mother's place has been sitting empty since she had the accident and they moved her into the physical therapy rehab center."

As much as she wanted to argue the payment arrangement, she couldn't afford to say no. It was a generous offer and would go a long way to helping her get her life back on track. *A true blessing*. Odd that it had come from David—but still, a blessing.

"Fine. Thank you. I will accept your generous offer, but on one condition."

"What's that?" One eyebrow rose. Being able to raise just one was something he'd always been able to do, and the expression on his usually serious face, one that used to make her laugh.

"That we keep boundaries between us." Ashley glanced down at Cory, double-checking that he wasn't listening. "I'm not looking to pick up where we left off, and I'm hoping you're not, either. Things didn't end well between us." It had to be said, just so they were both on the same page. No miscommunication this time.

"We're grownups, Ashley. And, no, I'm not looking for a relationship with you. Nothing's changed in my life. It wasn't right for me before, and it's still not. But it would be nice if we could be friends again. I've missed you."

Everything he said was good, right up until the last three words. *I've missed you.* It was an understatement when it came to Ashley's feelings about him. The shiver of hope rushing through her body was familiar, yet unwanted when it involved David.

"I don't know. Let me think about the friend thing. For now, just consider me your tenant. Even if I'm not paying rent and technically squatting." Ashley grinned, unable to resist. They had to find common ground if they were going to be living close to each other. David was being kind and deserved kindness in return.

The problem of where to stay was solved, and only time would tell how it would play out. Luckily, she'd be so busy trekking through the woods and searching for the eagle, it's not like she'd be around much anyway.

And with any luck, she'd get a job offer soon and be long gone, leaving Hallbrook and David behind. Again.

"You can squat at my place anytime," David joked. He meant what he'd said about being friends with her. He'd missed her. A lot. And the fact his pulse had raced into overdrive from the minute he spotted her standing in front of the cottage told him just how much.

"Lame." Ashley smiled. The sun was behind a cloud, but not where he was standing. Ashley had always been his sunshine.

"It was worth a try. If you follow me in the truck, I'll show you where I live."

"Thanks. I appreciate this. It has been a shock. And I'm trying not to let it bother me because I'm thankful Cory, Tricia, and I got out safely. I'd just finished unpacking the last of the boxes this morning. I didn't have a chance to get anything out of the house." David could tell she was struggling to be strong.

"My mother's place will have most of what you need in the way of essentials."

"Somehow, I doubt she has kid's clothes and toys and things like that. Unless she has a grandchild hidden away somewhere that I don't know about?" Ashley flashed him another one of her teasing smiles that warmed his heart.

David had fallen hard for her years ago, and he'd never been able to forget her. Ashley, on the other hand, didn't seem to have the same problem. For her, even friendship with him was a stretch.  The truth of her words still stung.

"Unfortunately, no. I told you I haven't changed, and I'm not cut out for a relationship. With anyone. So, no grandkids stashed away, much to my mother's disappointment." A flash of pain crossed her face, making him regret the words that served as a reminder of the past. He'd been a jerk to break it off with Ashley in high school without so much as an explanation or discussion. Just a cold-hearted statement of fact. But it had been the only way he could end things and not give in to the demands of his heart which told him walking away was a huge mistake. It had been the right thing to do, it just hadn't been easy.

"Come on, Cory. You need to climb into your car seat so I can buckle you in. We're going to follow Mr. David to our new temporary home." Ashley turned away, pulling Cory with her toward the car she'd parked on the street.

"Are we gonna stay with him? And Kojak? Yippee!" David heard the little boy's excitement and smiled. At least Cory was willing to be his friend.

Ashley retrieved a couple of items from the sidewalk and tossed them in the front seat of her car. He let Kojak hop in the truck, the dog immediately

going to the passenger side. David slid in the driver's seat and started the truck, pulling up next to
Ashley's vehicle to wait for her signal she was ready
to follow.

Minutes later, they headed toward his place. It
wasn't far and soon they were both turning into the
driveway, parking side by side. David didn't bother
pulling into the garage knowing the sounds and
vibrations of the garage door opening and closing
were the one thing his mother complained about
the place.  He'd learned early on not to use the
garage at night when his mother would already be
fast asleep. And he wouldn't use it now, so as not to
disturb his temporary residents.

He waited by the steps that led up to the top of
the garage, Kojak by his side. Cory ran up to greet
them both, Ashley a few steps behind, carrying
what looked like a couple of briefcases. "It looks like
you managed to salvage a few things?"

Ashley nodded. "I did. Luckily, my computer and
camera bag were at the door. I have a huge amount
of money tied up in my camera and the lenses, and
there's no way I could replace them. The computer,

on the other hand, has all my artwork and projects stored on it."

"Ever heard of the cloud?" David shook his head and smiled, unable to resist teasing her.

"As a matter of fact, wise guy, I have. I'm not in the dark ages, you know. But I worry someone could steal my photo if the system gets hacked."

"You always did have a problem trusting. For the most part, things are secure. I'm sure your files would be safe. Safer than if they'd been burned up in the fire."

Ashley flinched. "Point taken. Maybe I'll look into it." She turned away, ending the discussion.

"Let me take this for you." David reached for the larger of the two cases.

"I can handle my own bags," she said, pulling back.

For all the things that hadn't changed about Ashley, some things had. She didn't want help. It was as though she was trying to prove something. The question was, what? "I wasn't suggesting you can't. I simply thought you might want to hold Cory's hand as you go up the stairs."

"Oh, true," she said, clearly rattled. Ashley handed him one of the bags and took her son's hand. "Hold on to the rail, honey." Cory immediately did as she asked, happily trouncing up the stairs as he followed Kojak to the top.

Touchy and withdrawn, Ashley wasn't letting anyone close. She was also recently divorced and not rolling in dough. He was pretty sure he remembered her ex was big in the financial world. To see her living in the place she'd been renting, and then to hear her comment about her equipment, left him wondering more and more about what happened in California. Not because he was nosey, but because he cared. She deserved better.

David stopped at the top of the landing and removed the apartment key from his chain. He opened the door before turning back to hand her the key. "Here you go. I'm giving you mine to help put your worries about my intentions to rest. I won't have access to this place until you give me the key back. Or unless you invite me in." He grinned, holding the door open as they all went inside.

"Thank you. I wasn't worried. Trent assured me you're still a good guy." Ashley rewarded him with another one of her teasing smiles.

"Was there ever any doubt?" he asked, enjoying the banter.

"Yes." Ashley nodded, putting him in his place. So much for banter.

"The apartment is small, but it works well for my mother. Not as much to keep up with."

"What happened to her? If you don't mind my asking, that is." Ashley put her bag on the kitchen table, and David followed her lead.

"I don't mind. Mom was in a car accident, and her left hip and leg were crushed. The surgery was a difficult repair, and they put her in the physical therapy rehab center for a few months. She's doing well, just complaining of being somewhere other than her own home. She's kind of a homebody." It didn't help that the rehab center was in Lancaster, and David didn't get to see her nearly as often as he'd like. But he'd found the best facility in the area and was at least confident in their ability to help her heal. *Too bad they can't fix her broken heart.*

"It's great you were able to do this for her. You always did take good care of your mother since your father passed away." Ashley had no way of knowing the pain her words brought to the surface, even though his father's accident happened when he was sixteen.

He tamped down any response he'd been about to make, not letting his emotions run his mouth. "Yes, I built this apartment several years ago when I moved back here. I always hated working out of town and being away from her. When the job with the White Mountain Fire Department came up, I jumped at the chance to be closer. Especially since she was finding it more and more difficult to take care of her own place. As battalion chief, I'm able to have an office at any fire department in the district. I chose Hallbrook. Keeps me close to home and able to keep an eye on Mom every day."

After his father died, David had felt like it was his responsibility to watch over his mother. Not that he thought he did a good job she'd never really recovered from the tragedy. Time after time, he'd tried to get her into grief counseling, but she wouldn't listen.

Mother knew best, or at least she thought she did.

"That's great. What a blessing. And I'm so glad everything worked out for you and your career. I know you always wanted to be a firefighter."

It was true. His reasons may have changed, but not the heart he put into the job. "I'm going to see about putting a lift on the stairs so that when my mom comes home, she'll be able to get into the apartment easily."

"She's lucky to have you." Ashley watched him closely as if she wanted to say something more. The shuttered look that crossed her face seconds later was a clear indication that whatever it was would remain unspoken.

Cory raced around the room. "Mom, look at this." He pointed at the oversized rocker recliner, jumping in and rocking back and forth. "And look at this big TV." He was back out of the chair and grabbing the remote.

"No TV right now," Ashley said. There was so much love in her voice for the boy, and his answering shrug proved they had a close bond.

Cory set the remote back on the table and raced down the hall. He was back in minutes, his exuberance a bit faded. "Mommy, there's no kid bedroom. There's a huge grown-up bed, but there's only one. Where am I going to sleep?" he asked, his eyes wide with innocence.

"With me, silly. It's just for a little while." Ashley kissed the top of his head.

"Does that mean you'll pick up my toys since it's your room too?"

Ashley chuckled. "We'll figure something out. Maybe we can work together to keep our room clean."

"It will be easy now, won't it? Seeing as I don't have any toys." His blue eyes filled with tears. "Jackson was burned up in the fire."

"I'm sure he's in stuffed-bunny heaven, honey. You can snuggle with me until we find you another favorite bunny." Ashley hugged her son, brushing away the few tears that slid down onto his cheeks.

"Promise?" Cory seemed slightly mollified with the idea of a new animal to replace what had obviously been his favorite toy.

David would have to see what he could do about fixing the toy problem. Cory was such a great kid, and he didn't seem to ask for much.

Flipping the lights on in each room as he showed Ashley where everything was located, he left them on to make the place look more welcoming. He still couldn't believe she was here, in his mother's apartment. Hours ago, he hadn't even known Ashley was in town.

Being this close to her again, the familiar scent of jasmine assailed him. It was the same perfume he'd given her for her birthday ages ago. Knowing she still wore it struck a chord in him as he realized whatever had been between them, wasn't completely a thing of the past.

"If there's anything you need, just let me know. I stay busy with the fire department and in the community, but here's my private number if you need me for anything. Might be better than calling 9-1-1." He grinned, picked up a paper and pen from his mother's desk, jotted down his number, and handed it to Ashley.

"Thank you, David. You've been a blessing in what can only be described as a disastrous day." Ashley hugged him and he reciprocated, letting his arms go around her.

David pulled her close as he reveled in a moment he'd never thought to experience again. He remembered how hard it had been when Trent told him Ashley was getting married. He'd fought the urge to fly to California, wanting to stop her from making a mistake. To tell her it was all wrong. But of course, he'd never done anything of the sort, because he had nothing to offer.

His life was the fire department. And he could never ask Ashley to deal with the risks that came with his job. It had been his choice to honor his father and carry on his legacy, but that choice had cost him the woman he loved. Holding her in his arms again stirred up old feelings best forgotten but he'd deal with those later. Right now—it felt right.

"That means we will say our prayers for you tonight, Mr. David. Mommy always taught me blessings and prayers go hand in hand," Cory said, breaking into the moment.

Ashley stepped away, drying her eyes with the back of her hand. Her emotional level was at a breaking point and it was time he gave her some space. For both their sakes.

"That's very sweet. Prayers are always welcome." David smiled down at Cory. He could use all the prayers he could get because with Ashley in town, he was going to need strength to resist her and the feelings he'd long since locked away in his heart.

# Chapter Four

♥

D AVID HEADED BACK TO his own place and tried to find ways to keep busy. He took Kojak for a walk. Fixed the dripping sink. Took out the trash. Anything to keep from thinking about Ashley, and that after all these years, she was literally staying next door. It had been a sliver short of insanity to offer the apartment over the garage, knowing how he felt about her. Had always felt about her.

It was no surprise when the lead investigator called, and his early feedback suggested faulty wiring. David was almost positive it would also be the final conclusion of the investigation. With the old wiring, the place had been a fire trap. Chief Anderson was pushing for a new law, one that would require inspections on housing built prior to the new wiring codes. The cottage fire would be another case his boss could use as evidence to prove why the change was necessary, something David was totally on board with. Just knowing Ashley and her son could have been hurt or killed in a house fire, gutted him. Thankfully, the fire broke out in the daytime and they'd acted quickly to get out of the place.

David shoved the what-if's out of his head that had been playing on repeat mode ever since he left Ashley. What he needed was to get back to work. He drove to the station and headed straight for his office. Powering up his computer, he started to fill out the reports he needed to file regarding the fire.

Not enough to keep him busy for long, he turned his focus to the upcoming prescribed burn he'd been planning for months. This usually wasn't an ideal time of the year because weather conditions were rarely ripe to implement the plan, but current indications were pointing to a window of opportunity.

One the fire department needed to take advantage of before the upcoming July 4th festivities. Lots of campers and a large number of hikers out on the trails, meant more opportunities for mistakes when it came to cigarettes and campfires. That led to an increased danger for a forest fire. A firefighter's worse nightmare.

Redirecting his focus only worked for so long. Soon, the people of Hallbrook started calling and stopping by the station. Within hours of the fire at the old cottage, everyone had learned what happened, and either wanted information or to know how they could help.

Margie Hatfield, the owner of the cottage, was one of the first to call. She'd immediately asked about the tenants. She was a kind woman with a huge heart, and even without knowing what had started the fire, her concern had been for Ashley and Cory.

David casually mentioned Cory had no toys and that neither Ashley nor her son had any clothes. Margie instantly went to work, putting out the word. In Hallbrook, the gossip chain sometimes worked miracles, and in this case, the miracles came in the form of food, clothes, and toys.

All of which were dropped off at the fire department, of course. Because the one thing he hadn't mentioned right away to Margie or anyone else, was the fact Ashley was living over his garage. The rumor mill would be all too quick to remember they'd once dated and would start to speculate. It was something he wanted to put off for as long as possible.

Now, not even twenty-four hours later, David was back on her doorstep, his arms loaded with the first of many boxes he needed to deliver, including one very special delivery he'd gone out of his way to pick out himself.

David balanced the delivery on his knee to free up one hand. *Knock. Knock.* Securing the box again, he stepped back to wait.

The door opened, and Ashley stood there in his mother's pink robe and fluffy white slippers, her brown, curly hair still messy from what could only have been a restless night judging by the disarray.

She cinched the belt tighter, her hands then going to the lapels and clutching them as if they were a security blanket. "Good morning. I didn't expect to see you here this early. Or at all."

What Ashley didn't know, and would never know, was that he loved the fresh-out-of-bed look. She would be beautiful no matter what time of day or hairstyle. "I won't be here long. I come bearing gifts."

Ashley let out a deep sigh. "David, I thought we talked about this. I don't want to be obligated to you for anything." Her voice quivered as she said the last words, revealing far more pain than she'd probably intended. He knew he'd hurt her, but this was seeing it firsthand and far too many years later.

It was difficult having her back in town, but it would be worse if he thought there was a chance she still cared for him. That would be disastrous for them both. "Then you'll be happy to know this isn't from me. The people in town dropped off some things at the fire station for you and Cory." He gazed down at the box and then back at her, waiting for her to tell him where to put it.

"Oh. In that case, can you set the box on the table? It looks like there's food in there, which is a huge relief. There's not much in your mom's place to choose from. Not that I'm complaining. I really appreciate you letting us stay here." Her comment was uttered with a sigh of relief. He didn't want to dwell on the difference. Not here and now, anyway.

"I see you found my mother's robe. You look like a fluffy bunny." *A sweet, adorable bunny.*

"Pink was never my color," Ashley said, glancing down before looking back at him, a frown on her face.

"Purple was always your favorite." Not that he didn't like the pink.

"You remember that?" she asked, her eyebrows shooting up in surprise.

"Of course. I remember everything about you." It was the truth. Although, perhaps not the best response he could give considering the situation.

Ashley snorted. "Yeah, right. You seemed to have no problem going off to college and forgetting me." And just like that, the hurt was back in her eyes. Eyes that had always been expressive, like a window to her soul. She was still hurting over the past.

*That makes two of us.* "Ashley, let's not go down memory lane. It will serve no purpose at this point."

"Sure enough." A shuttered look crossed her face as she stepped back. "Thanks for stopping by. It was kind of everyone to chip in and help."

David rolled his eyes. "You have no idea." He welcomed the redirect back to the purpose of his visit.

"What's that supposed to mean?" she asked.

"Wait here." He headed for the door. Ashley was in for a surprise if she thought one box was the sum total of her gifts. *More like six.*

One by one, he carried the boxes up and set them on the table. "That's it," he said when he delivered the final box.

"I can't believe what I'm seeing. The people from town sent all this?" Ashley asked, completely stunned.

"Yes. And I have a feeling they aren't done yet. Once they get behind a project, all bets are off. And right now, you're the project." He winked.

"This is amazing." Ashley's eyes welled up with tears. "I didn't expect this."

"A long time ago, you were a part of this town. People remember and still care about you."

"They do, don't they?" She brushed the tears away with the sleeve of his mother's robe.

"I'm sure you'll find everything you need in these boxes, judging by what I saw being dropped off—toys, clothes, shoes, toiletries. I can't imagine they've forgotten anything. Oh, and I have one very special delivery. He located the box he'd tucked Cory's gift into, opened it, and handed Ashley the stuffed animal. "This is for Cory." He grinned.

"You got him a new bunny? That's terribly sweet of you." A fresh wave of tears rolled down her cheeks.

"It's no big deal. I just felt bad he lost his favorite bunny. Hopefully, this one will do."

"He'll love it. Thank you. Can I get you a cup of coffee?" Ashley offered.

David did a double take. He wanted to—more than he was willing to admit. But staying was the last thing he should do, second only to inviting her to stay here in the first place. Walking away when they were younger had been the hardest thing he'd ever done, and David wasn't sure he'd have the willpower to do it again. "Thanks, but I can't stay. I've got a full day of work ahead of me."

Ashley flinched, the hurt expression in her eyes a painful reminder of the past. It was like deja vu. And not his finest moment.

"Okay, just one cup. Thank you for offering," David relented, putting Ashley's needs in front of his own.

"I don't mean to be such an emotional wreck." She smiled up at him. A shy smile, but one that made him want to kiss her. Something he wouldn't do.

"I think if anyone's entitled, you are." David leaned against the counter as Ashley turned on the coffee pot.

"You mean because I'm divorced?" There was a tinge of resentment in her voice, but at least they were talking. It was a step in the right direction considering their history together.

"No. Because you just moved across the country, got settled in, and then had a fire that drove you from your new place and robbed you of everything you owned. That's a lot for anyone to go through." He was trying to sympathize with her, but she'd immediately jumped to the wrong conclusion.

Clearly, she was sensitive about her divorce. It wasn't the first time her comments left him wondering what really happened in California. It had to be significant for her to leave the state with her son, driving clear across the country to start over. And what did that say of her ex-husband? The man didn't seem to care that she'd taken Cory with her.

She let out a deep sigh, something he noticed her doing far too often. "True. Thanks." She shrugged.

"Still don't want the world to see your vulnerability, do you? There's nothing wrong with needing help now and then." David pressed to see if she'd share. Once upon a time, they'd shared everything. Well, almost everything. He'd never told her about watching his father die. Or watching his mother live as though she wished she'd died with his father.

"You're one to talk. The man who doesn't believe in relationships. The man who doesn't let anyone get too close." Ashley had turned the tables on him without so much as a blink of the eye.

"I let you get close." He said, not liking the direction of the conversation.

Ashley's sharp gaze left him squirming. "And then you walked away."

"Point taken. So, are you in town for long?" David wasn't sure how he wanted to her answer but steeled himself for her response either way.

Ashley handed him the first cup of coffee and then popped in the second k-cup to brew another. "Probably not. I've applied to a few places for work, but I'm hoping to get in with National Geographic. They're looking for a new photographer." Her face lit up as she mentioned her dream job.

"That's all you could talk about when you were younger. It's awesome you might get an opportunity to work with them. I'm sure you'll get it." He took a sip of coffee, enjoying the bold chicory flavor.

"I don't want to get my hopes too high. It's a competitive job, and I'm sure there are people way more qualified than me trying to get it."

"I've seen your work. You're an amazing photographer, and your talent shines through in every picture you take. It's like the photo is a piece of your heart."

Ashley looked up at him in shock. "When have you seen my work?"

"Trent is proud of you. Anything you've ever sent him is hanging on the walls at his house. Between the two of us, you have quite the admiration society." David smiled. It was nothing more than the truth.

Ashley's answering blush touched his heart. Still the same sweet, not overly confident Ashley she'd always been. "Thanks. I had no idea Trent was that interested in my work." Did she leave him out because she knew he was a fan, or because she didn't want to think about it? Either way, it probably didn't matter. Or it needed to be left alone. To go there would mean getting too close to the past.

"You'd be surprised. Trent has always been protective and proud of his little sister." It was Trent's protective side that David had dealt with back in high school. Even as best friends, Trent had been clear David wasn't good enough for her. No one was in his eyes.

"Yes, that's true. Trent goes overboard, or at least he used too far too often. After our dad died, he sort of designated himself as my keeper. And when mom passed, his being away at college didn't stop him from his duties, it only magnified them. Trent used to call me every day. It was nice, but also frustrating and embarrassing."

"I remember, trust me." But that wasn't something he was willing to discuss with Ashley. The past was best left in the past. David had let Trent push him away from her, but it only worked because he'd been looking for a way out anyway. Life hadn't worked out for David and Ashley to have a happily-ever-after.

"If you're looking for work elsewhere, what brings you back to Hallbrook? Trent?"

"Actually, some volunteer work." Ashley grabbed her cup when the gurgling sound of the coffeemaker stopped, and then she came to sit at the table with him. David moved one of the boxes to make room for her.

"What kind of work?" he asked, happy to be back in a safer conversation.

"It's actually a pretty cool deal. There's been a reported sighting of a bald eagle near here, and the Audubon Society called me to check it out. They knew I used to live in Hallbrook and know the area. I'm trying to find the eagle and nest as part of the Bald Eagle Project in New Hampshire." Ashley's excitement came spilling out with each sentence. It was a fantastic opportunity for her.

"That sounds awesome and right up your alley. Just think, if you find it, there might be a National Geographic media spread. Eagles are big news. Where was the reported sighting?"

"We don't exactly know. The people were hiking when they noticed him flying overhead. They were in the White Mountains Forest, mentioned a large pond, and listed their proximity to Hallbrook and the North Summit parking lot as the exit point of their hike. That's pretty much all they could tell us. I'm going to mark out the area on the map and set up gridded sections to play eagle scout." She grinned. "Of course, there's the added bonus of any other wildlife photos I get along the way."

David winced. He was thrilled for Ashley, but there was one little problem. Make that a big problem. "You'll need to get a move on with your search. You probably don't know this yet, seeing as you've only just arrived back in town, but the fire department has a prescribed burn tentatively scheduled. We've been waiting on ideal weather conditions, and it looks like we might get them in about five days. If the weather conditions hold out, we need to move forward with the burn."

Ashley shook her head, her brow drawn tight. "But you can't burn anything if there's an eagle nest out there."

"I understand that. But as of now, there are no confirmed nests, are there?" he asked, knowing the answer.

"Can't you wait until I finish my search?"

"No. We've been waiting for months. Ideal conditions don't come around very often, and we really hope to have this done before the summer."

"But the eagle deserves a chance to establish his home and deserves the protection due an eagle in our country. I realize they are no longer on the endangered species list, but they are still the symbol of our country, representing freedom and strength. And just because they aren't on the list now, doesn't mean we can let down our guard or they'll be right back on the list. You can't burn. Please," Ashley begged.

"I get that you want to protect the eagles. I'm all for it. But I have to consider the bigger picture. Our number one objective is to reduce the fuel available in the event of a forest fire. This is about protecting our community, not just one eagle."

Ashley bit down on her lip, fighting back the urge to argue her point. He knew the look all too well.

"I'm sorry. I should leave. I've got work to do." David stood, moving to the sink to rinse out his cup before setting it on the counter.

"You wouldn't happen to have a map of the park, would you? If I have limited time, I need to get started out there today. My original gridded map was lost in the fire." Ashley's clipped voice made it clear she wasn't happy he wouldn't do things her way.

"Sure thing. I'm betting I have a couple in the truck." David headed downstairs to get her a map. Anything to help her cause. He honestly did support her efforts. There were only fifty-nine pairs of bald eagles currently recorded in the state of New Hampshire. Umbagog Lake had more than its fair share, and it would be great if they could lay claim to one right here near Hallbrook.

An eagle's nest would be federally protected, as well as the area surrounding them. But until Ashley found one, his hands were tied. The community and the forest had to come first, and the burn had to move forward.

He walked back into the apartment and handed Ashley the map. "Good luck. I hope you find what you're looking for."

"Thanks," Ashley said, looking like there was more on her mind.

"Mommy?" Cory's sleepy voice called from the back bedroom.

She needed to go, and continuing the conversation was pointless. "Looks like duty calls for both of us. Don't forget to phone me if you need anything." David walked out the door, not bothering to wait for an answer.

# Chapter Five

♥

TRUE TO HIS WORD, David only dropped by to bring in more boxes of donations. The outpouring of love from the community continued to soften her heart and make her feel welcome. Like she was home. At first, she'd felt like a charity case, but no matter how much she told people in town that she had plenty, they just kept sending more. It was like it made them happy to help. There was a real sense of community that she'd missed since moving to a big city.

Cory had more toys now than what she'd brought from California, and he was in his element. What little boy wouldn't be overjoyed with Christmas in July? He'd named his new bunny Jax, short for Jackson. The sentimentality behind Cory's choice was another example of her son's huge heart. Jax was his new bed-time buddy to snuggle with, and David, of course, his new best friend for giving Cory the bunny.

The only thing he wasn't happy about nowadays was how little he saw Kojak. He'd always wanted a dog, but Joe had been adamant against it. In hindsight, considering what had happened between her and her ex-husband, that had been a good thing. It'd been hard enough coming across the country with Cory and all their belongings in a U-Haul trailer and towing her car behind them. Bringing a dog would have been inconceivable. Not to mention the added difficulty of trying to find a place to rent that took pets, and even if they did, the added expense.

"Hey, Mommy. Look." Cory's finger was pressed to the window as he faced her. The excitement in his voice could only mean one thing—Kojak was in the backyard. Ashley moved to the window, knowing it was important to share in his joy. She laughed as she watched the dog chase a ball until she realized who was doing the throwing.

David came into view, and her gaze trailed him instead of Kojak and his antics. He threw the ball and hollered at the dog to fetch it. This was a David she hadn't seen in a long time. A laughing, smiling David. Once upon a time, he'd been like that with her. *Best friends.*

She'd never admit it to anyone other than herself, but it still hurt to think about the way they'd separated. Common courtesy would have at least dictated they discuss the breakup, considering it wasn't like anything bad had happened between them. No fights. No incident. Nothing. David had simply pulled her aside after school one day and announced it was over between them, telling her he was going away to college. He'd claimed he didn't want to give her the wrong impression that there would ever be a future between them.

What kind of a breakup was that? The kind that ripped a girl's heart out. The kind that left her cold and crying in the privacy of their bedroom at night.

It had almost been a welcome relief when David and Trent had gone off to college, leaving her behind. Better not to see David. And where Trent was, David was close at hand. It would seem the two were best friends for life.

It had also been a blessing each time Trent came home from school and David stayed away. Seeing him would have been a painful reminder of her broken heart and dreams. To a lesser extent, that was what was happening now. Luckily, she was over him. *Mostly.*

Life could have been so different. But it did no good to think about it now, and besides, she had her son. And she'd do everything in her life all over again to have Cory. Move to California after her mother died. Marry Joe. In truth, even the divorce was a blessing, because now she could raise Cory the way she wanted to, without Joe's interference.

Ashley turned away from the window, but not before David looked up and waved, catching them in the act of gawking. "Time for breakfast, Cory."

"Can we have pancakes this morning?" She was surprised he hadn't asked to go down and play with David and Kojak. Apparently, his hunger was greater than his need for doggy time.

"Yes, of course." It was his favorite breakfast, not to mention hers as well. Ever since she'd found a healthy but delicious way to make them, she couldn't get enough. Moist and nutty, the cottage cheese and yogurt pancakes were always a hit with everyone who tried them.

"Yummy, yummy in my tummy." He giggled, and the sound was music to Ashley's ears.

She pulled all the ingredients from the refrigerator and pantry, the supplies all a reminder of the community's generosity. Later today, she needed to run into town and drop off the portfolio she'd put together at the request of the National Geographic's human resource department. She still couldn't believe the email she'd received yesterday, even though she'd read it at least twenty times already. Being under consideration was a huge step forward.

While Cory ate his breakfast, Ashley packed her backpack for today's outing. In the past three days, she'd managed to mark off three of the sixteen gridded areas, each one covering a square mile. With each day, Ashley had been hopeful to spot the eagle or find the nest. And each day, she'd returned home disappointed. The only upside was the beautiful photos she'd taken capturing wildlife, unique foliage, and blossoms, some of which she planned to add to her collection of favorites.

Thirty minutes later, she was ready to go. Cory was eager to go play with Tricia's children and her niece and nephew. It had been a blessing when Tricia had volunteered to watch him while she went trekking through the woods. Kids weren't always the quietest or the easiest to keep from getting bored on a nature walk.

"So, what's the plan for today?" Tricia asked. Her friend liked to know what area Ashley was searching and then backed up the information with a photo of the grid. It was overly cautious, but it was nice to have someone worry about her for a change. It had been so long; she'd forgotten what that felt like.

"I've got to stop in town at the post office, but then I'm going to try and knock out this section. And if possible, this one." She opened the map and pointed at the gridded areas she planned to visit. "Thank you so much for doing this."

Tricia snapped two photos. "I just wish I could do more. It won't be long before my house is back to normal. If things are still uncomfortable where you are, you can come and stay here for a bit. Not much space, but lots of fun." She laughed.

"Thanks for the offer. I'm doing okay. It helps to keep busy. Call me if you need anything. So far, I haven't lost cell service out there."

"Take your time, I'm sure the kids will be fine."

"Be good for Miss Tricia, honey. Love you." Ashley kissed the top of her son's head.

"Bye, Mommy." He hugged her leg and then ran off, eager to play with the other kids.

Ashley left and drove toward the post office. She pulled into a spot directly in front of the small brick building. The American flag flew high and proud on the pole out front, the wind causing it to ripple gently.

She crossed the scuffed tiled floor that had seen better days and entered through the interior glass door to the smaller area where the postal business was transacted. "Hi, Mrs. Adams," Ashley said, surprised to see the older woman still working here. "I need to mail this package, please. Do you have a photo label we can add to the envelope to alert mail staff to be a little more careful with it?"

"Of course, dearie. I heard you were back in town. And I heard about the fire. My goodness, that must have been awful. Is David taking good care you?"

Rachael Adams was a kindly woman with access to all the current gossip just by showing up to work each day.

Having people link her and David together wasn't good. Better she nix the idea now than let the rumor mill go crazy. "I'm not staying with David. My son, Cory, and I are staying in his mother's apartment. We are taking care of ourselves and doing great, all things considered. The town has been very generous and supportive, for which I'm very appreciative."

"David's a nice, attractive young man. You two are older now, but I remember when you dated. So cute together." Mrs. Adams was heading down memory lane, a place Ashley had no intention of going.

"All history. There's nothing between us now. Trust me," Ashley said, hoping to reinforce the idea and wipe away any lingering doubts as to the status between her and David.

The older woman stuck four photo labels on the envelope, and then put it on the scale to check for the postage due. "I reckon you're coming to the festival next week, right? The whole town will be there, and I'm sure you can get reacquainted. It would give you a chance to tell folks thank you in person."

"I'd forgotten about that until I saw one of the posters. I remember how much fun the Independence Day festival was, and I'm looking forward to taking Cory." Cotton candy. Games. Balloons. Food galore. Rides. Her son would love it all.

"You know, they're looking for volunteers. Would be nice if you could help. I'm sure the committee would love to have you." Mrs. Adams grinned, her smile revealing a few missing teeth.

"I don't know if I'll have time, what with Cory, and searching for the bald eagle." Ashley shrugged, unsure how she could possibly add more to her schedule.

"I heard about the search. Would be right special if you found a pair of nesting eagles.  I reckon it would bring a lot of attention to our little town, and maybe some more business to the area. Glen Haven is growing, and we need to keep up."

"Thanks, I'm hoping to find one, but it's not easy. Just say a prayer for me." Ashley ran her credit card to pay for the postage.

"Well, just think about helping. Every little bit is welcome." The older woman took her package and dropped it in a bin with other envelopes.

*It would be nice if she gave back to the people in town.* Ashley got as far as the front door before she made up her mind. The community had opened their arms and helped her and Cory out when they needed it. That's what the spirit of giving and love was all about. It was something she wanted to make sure her son understood as he grew up, and there was no better way to show him than by doing it. Actions always spoke louder than words. And it wasn't like the Audubon Society was paying her, so there wasn't a deadline. Other than David and the fire department, that is.

Ashley stopped and turned back to Mrs. Adams. "Who do I talk to about signing up if I want to help?" *She'd make it work. Somehow.*

"That would be Sally Little over at her diner. You remember her?"

"Of course." Ashley smiled. "Best peach pie in the county. Who could forget that?"

"True. It's nice to have you back in town, dearie."

"Thank you, Mrs. Adams. Good to see you again. And if you get a chance, pray for the weather to change for the worse." She grinned.

"Whatever for? We're about to have wonderful weather. I'm hoping these pleasant temperatures hold out for the festival."

There wasn't time to stick around and explain. "Never mind," Ashley said, waving as she left. Turning right, she headed down the sidewalk toward Sally's. Peach pie sounded delicious, but not for breakfast. Luckily, she had pancakes this morning, or she might have been tempted. Maybe later this afternoon, she'd bring Cory here for a treat.

Ashley entered Sally's, the cowbells overhead jingling to announce her arrival. She immediately spotted Sally behind the counter. The woman was full of smiles and good cheer, and always willing to chat with her customers. Some things never changed.

Ashley picked one of the counter stools to sit. The red leather cushion, cracked and worn with age, was like the rest of the place—a little worn and outdated—but the diner still had plenty of regular customers, and the place was half full for breakfast.

"Good morning, Mrs. Little," Ashley said when Sally handed her a menu.

"I don't believe I... Oh, wait, I do know you. I didn't recognize you for a second, Ashley Anderson. Heard you were back in town. Oh, and the fire. You poor thing. I'm so glad the town chipped in and took care of you. Haven't seen that brother of yours this past week, what's he doing? And call me Sally, for heaven's sake. You're not a child anymore." The woman talked faster than an auctioneer selling cattle, and it was hard to get a word in edgewise.

"It's Stanton now. I was married, and I have a four-year-old son, Cory. As to Trent, he's off on some business trip and supposed to be back in a few days." Ashley smiled.

"Well, you tell Trent I got some peach pie waiting for him. He's one of my best customers. That boy has got quite the appetite, and he likes to bring Maria here. The two are goo-goo over each other and my pie." Sally winked as if she'd just told Ashley a colossal secret. But everyone knew there were no secrets in Hallbrook.

"I'll tell him. I was just talking to Mrs. Adams, and she told me you need more people to help set up the festival. Everyone's been so kind, and I'd love a chance to return some of their generosity."

"Oh, that's wonderful, dear. I've got the chart all set up to organize the teams. And I've got the perfect place to add you. Oh, and we're having a committee meeting this afternoon at three. Can you be here?" Sally gazed at her, the question more of a "be there", not a "can you be there."

"Three? I can make it work." She'd planned on covering two sections, but this was for a good cause. She'd have to come back early today and cover less area and then try to do more tomorrow. Although, she also didn't want to take advantage of Tricia's generosity and have Cory stay at her place all day, every day.

"That would be wonderful, honey. I'm going to go over all the details and give everybody their assignments. Then each of the teams will have a chance to meet and discuss what they need to do amongst themselves to make their tasks easier. If everyone does their small share, the whole project will come together beautifully."

"It sounds like you've got quite a handle on this," Ashley said, nodding. Sally Little was iconic in

Hallbrook for her organizational talents in the past, but this went well beyond.

"I can't take all the credit." Sally beamed. "I've been setting the festival up for twenty years, but now we have an event coordinator in town by the name of Gemma Duncan. She's the one who knows how to organize like nobody's business. We've teamed up together, and she's helping me to manage this year. It's been so much easier." Sally moved to fill two glasses of soda and dropped them off to the couple sitting a few seats away.

"Sounds perfect. I can't wait to meet Miss Duncan." The sleepy little town was growing if it needed an event coordinator.

"Mrs. Duncan. Her husband's the handsome doctor in town. He's been here almost five years, I reckon. If you or Cory need any medical help, see Dr. Jake Duncan. You'll be in good hands." Sally Little was turning out to be a wealth of information. "Can I get you anything to eat?"

"I already ate at home this morning. I should run, but thanks for all the information. I'll see you at three."

"Sounds good." Sally picked up a tab and waved.

Ashley waved back and headed for the door. Twenty minutes later, she pulled into the North Summit parking lot that was closest to the area she intended to search today. She strapped on the backpack she'd loaded with her standard hiking gear. Water and power bars, tissues, a first aid kit, her phone, a spare battery pack, a notebook, and a pen. She attached her compass to a belt loop and opened the map.

Following the main trail, she took short side journeys, always marking her location and returning to the main path. Her hiking boots were a lifesaver, saving her a few times as she tripped over raised tree roots. Always on the lookout for any sign of the eagle, she searched the skies and the trees, stopping periodically to use her binoculars to look high up in the tall pine trees. An eagle's nest was massive, but typically well hidden.

The sun-spotted leaves cast flickering shadows on the ground, and the air was cooler under the blanket of cover. Ashley stopped to grab a few pinecones to take home to Cory. It would be fun to use for an arts and crafts project. She remembered making animals out of them when she was a little girl, using colorful pipe cleaners, construction paper, and cotton.

A woodpecker tapped on a tree nearby, and Ashley searched for the origin of the heavy thudding sound. She was rewarded when she spotted a pileated woodpecker, one of her favorites. More memories flooded her brain, thinking of all the times she'd caught a glimpse of them and then hunted them down with her camera. All in an effort to capture an elusive award-winning shot.

The air was fresh and clean, and Ashley felt at peace with the great outdoors. She snapped a few pictures along the way, capturing some of the other birds, foliage, and mountain blossoms. She was extremely pleased when she spotted a fox running through the woods who stopped just long enough to check her out, giving her time to take a photo.

After several hours, she stopped to eat a power bar and have another drink of water. She glanced at her watch and realized she needed to head back to town soon. It wouldn't be right to be late for the meeting after she'd just promised to be there.

Ashley blotted out another gridded area with tiny X's to mark today's coverage. She came to an opening that looked out over a large pond. The place reminded her of the description in the report of the sighting. But there were hundreds of ponds in this area.

The stillness of the woods and peaceful air made the view breathtaking. Ashley stopped to drink in the sunshine and savor the moment. This was part of what she loved best about the woods. The fresh pine scent, the peaceful sounds of birds singing, the squirrels rustling in the leaves as they gathered food and played. Nature was one of God's beautiful creations, and the woods were one of Ashley's favorite places to explore.

Off in the distance, she spotted several large birds soaring through the air, taking advantage of the air current. Her heart beat faster, although she knew from experience, they were more than likely turkey vultures based on the pattern they flew. But until confirmed, there was always the chance. She lifted her binoculars and focused, zooming in on them.

Turkey vultures. Just as she'd suspected. Ashley was disappointed, but still, even the vultures were fascinating birds when one considered their size and impact on the ecosystem.

She turned and started to make her way toward where she'd parked, circling back on a lower path to cover more territory. A screeching bird call reached her ears and Ashley stopped, searching the sky. The sound was remarkably like an eagle's cry.

Wishful thinking wouldn't turn it into an eagle. It could have also been a hawk or an osprey. It was challenging for an untrained ear to tell the screeches apart. Ashley marked the spot on her map, anxious to continue her exploration of the area tomorrow. She started to leave, but a red splash of color caught her attention. And then another. And another. Ashley moved closer to inspect and discovered they were flags. A sick feeling settled in the pit of her stomach.

The twenty-foot-wide path that had been dug and cleared increased her concern, but it was the logo of the White Mountain Fire Department that confirmed her suspicions. *It was the boundary of the burn.* After the meeting, she'd have to find David and get him to fix this. There was no way they could burn here until she'd finished her search.

Ashley snatched up one of the flags and shoved it in her camera bag. She was already going to be fifteen minutes late to the meeting, but considering her discovery, it was well worth breaking one of her own rules.

# Chapter Six

♥

ASHLEY WALKED IN THROUGH the double doors of the community center. The parking lot had been full, but judging by the buzz of voices coming from the meeting room, her late entry wasn't a problem. Sally Little was in the middle of the room talking to a group of people, and Ashley headed her way to check-in.

"Hey, Sally, sorry I'm late. I got caught up with a possible eagle sighting just as I was about to leave the woods. I hope I didn't miss anything." She smiled at the jovial woman who seemed to be in her element this evening.

"Don't worry. You missed the general information, but you're just in time for the team meetings. I've already given out everybody's spots, and your partner just arrived. There's three of you on the team, but your brother is one of them, and you said he won't be here for a few days." *Must have been a short and to-the-point meeting.*

For a sleepy little town, things moved promptly on schedule. But it also meant Ashley didn't have a clue what was going on, and she'd have to rely on the other teammate to catch her up. "Who's the other team member besides Trent?"

"I am," David said, coming to stand next to her. She hadn't noticed him when she arrived, which was unusual. Normally, her internal radar went off when he was near.

"What? Did you have something to do with this, David?" Ashley wouldn't put it past him.

"Hardly." He shrugged.

Sally shook her head, glancing back and forth between them. "I put together the teams. Ashley, I thought with you just arriving back in town, you might prefer to work with your brother. And since the three of you were all close friends, I decided you were the perfect trio for a team."

This wasn't what she signed on for. She'd rather work with anyone *but* David. He'd been nice to her, it was true, but it didn't wipe away the past or the sudden racing of her heart whenever he was near. Better to nix any resurgence of her feelings right away. "But—"

"No buts, young lady. You three will be fine. It's just the two of you right now until Trent gets back, so you two can decide the what, when, who, and Trent is stuck with whatever tasks you assign him. He can do the dirty work." She grinned. "His penalty for not being here tonight. I've got lots of people to talk to, so here's your list of things to do." Sally handed Ashley the paper and walked away, leaving Ashley no chance of convincing the woman to change her mind.

"Are you okay with this? If not, I'll work on it by myself until Trent gets here." *David the martyr.* She wasn't the only one sky-writing his lack of interest in spending time with her.

"Are you saying I'm not capable of pulling my weight?" Ashley pressed, unwilling to let him paint her as someone who didn't follow through on their promises. *Unlike him.*

"I just don't want you to be uncomfortable." David shrugged, his meaning clear. He didn't want her help, which was even more reason for her to do the opposite.

"I'm doing this to help the community. And if that means working with you, then I'll do it. It's not like there's anything between us personally, so working with you means nothing. It will be no different than if I was working with Trent." Not exactly, but Ashley didn't want him to know that. She was strong and independent, and she could do this. Rise to the occasion. Something she hadn't been strong enough to do when she was sixteen, letting him walk away without a fight. They may have only dated for six months, but she'd loved him for years.

His left eyebrow shot up in disbelief. "Fine. Then let's do this," David said. "How about I come by your place tonight at six, and we go over the list and break down the details?" She was tempted to tease him about his eyebrow thing, something she'd done lots of time in the past, but she wasn't quite in the teasing mood.

"Don't you mean your place?" Ashley asked. Technically, the garage apartment was his. Or at least his mother's.

"It's your place for as long as you're living there. We've already established that." David waited for an answer, his gaze never leaving her face.

"Fine. Bring pizza." She could do this. Would do this, in fact. Besides, it was the perfect opportunity to discuss the flags she'd found today. Pizza and persuasion were on the dinner menu. David just didn't know it yet.

David pulled into his driveway and grabbed the box of pizza from the backseat. He made a quick stop to let Kojak out for a potty break, but instead of putting the dog back in the house, he led him up the stairs to Ashley's place. Cory loved the dog, and it would help reduce tension between him and Ashley. Win-win decision the way he saw it.

Having her on his volunteer team wasn't ideal, but he'd make the best of the situation. It was important in his position to be a part of the community, and that meant he couldn't back out. He'd been more than a little surprised when she'd agreed to his suggestion for tonight, figuring she'd counter his offer with one of her own. Like a public meeting at O'Malley's. More than likely, it was more convenient for her and Cory to meet here.

Other than donation drop-offs, he hadn't seen her. He was busy getting ready for the burn, and she was busy searching for the bald eagle. This morning had been the first time he didn't have a box to deliver, and he'd found himself missing the early morning greeting and the sight of her beautiful face. He knocked on the door and didn't have to wait long before Ashley opened it.

"Right on time, I see," she said, glancing at her watch.

"That's true. But then I remember a certain girl once read me the riot act when I was late a couple of times. I learned a valuable lesson when I was younger." He grinned and stepped into the apartment.

"Nice to know I was good for something." She shrugged.

"You are good for a lot of things. Don't sell yourself short. I'm the one who had the issues. Trust me." It was nothing short of the truth, and he owed her that much. It's not like he'd been overly forthcoming when he'd broke it off. But how did a guy tell the girl he loved they had no future together? That his fate was tied to his father's legacy, and he couldn't let her be a part of his life because he knew the cost she'd pay if anything went wrong His mother was living proof and a constant reminder of what could happen to those left behind.

"Here, let me take the pizza." She reached for the box, changing the subject. Perhaps it was for the best. Wandering into the past wouldn't be helpful to either one of them at this point. Water under the bridge. The only thing that hadn't drifted away with the current of time was his feelings for her.

Cory came running into the room, a huge smile on his face when he spotted Kojak. "You brought him! Hey, buddy, I missed you." Cory dropped to his knees and hugged the dog.

"I did, but only as long as your mother doesn't mind." David looked up at her for confirmation.

"Of course, I don't mind. It's not every day Cory gets to play with a fire dog," she teased, her attitude becoming lighter the minute her son waltzed in the room.

"And it's not every day Kojak gets to play with a handsome young lad." David ruffled the kid's hair.

Hair the same color as his mothers. It had always reminded David of dark chocolate syrup. His favorite dessert sauce, of course.

"Just no throwing stuff in the house. We wouldn't want to break anything and I'm sure when Mrs. Beckett returns home, she'd like it intact," Ashley said, using her kind but firm mother voice.

"What's in tact?" Cory's questioning gaze causing his forehead to scrunch. David hadn't been around kids much other than at festivals and educational experiences offered at the elementary school and at the fire department. It was a fresh view to see life through a child's eyes. To see the simplicity of it all.

"Intact is one word, and it means to leave something the same way you found it. In this case, his mother has a right to expect her home to be the same way as she left it."

"Why'd she leave?" Cory asked.

"She had an accident and hurt her hip."

"Is it all better now?" Cory pressed for more information, his four-year-old quest for information cute. But then David wasn't the one who had to play twenty questions with the kid on a regular basis if this was the norm.

Ashley shook her head. "My goodness, you're full of questions tonight. Mr. David says she's getting all better, and when she's all healed, she'll come back here. And that's why we've got to find another place to live."

"All, shucks. I like it here. Maybe his mother could just live with us."

David grinned. Neither his mother nor Ashley would like that option. Although it might be good for his mother. "That's certainly something you could ask her if you meet her."

Ashley shook her head. "Don't fill him with any ideas. Cory, why don't you go play with Kojak in the living room where I can keep an eye on you. Mr. David and I need to talk about the July 4$^{th}$ festival. You can even have your pizza out there, but don't feed it to the dog."

Cory's eyes lit with excitement. Eating in the living room must be a big treat for the kid. "Okay, Mommy. Sorry, Kojak. No pizza for you." Cory rubbed the dog's head.

"Cute kid. Inquisitive," David said, watching the pair of them play in the living room, Cory rolling on the ground with the dog.

"They get to be that way around this age. It's non-stop questions. About everything." Ashley took a piece of pizza from the box and put it on a plate.

"When does he start school?" David grabbed a couple of napkins and followed her into the living room to deliver Cory's dinner.

"He's a late-year birthday, which puts him right on the border of where he might have been able to go this September, but I'm thinking of waiting until next year to give him a chance to be my little boy a year longer and to mature for kindergarten. His attention span might not be what a teacher with twenty other kids in a classroom can handle."

"I'm sure you know Cory better than anyone. If you think it's better to wait, then you should. And if you're still planning on leaving Hallbrook, it would be hard to start him in a school and then uproot him right away. Better to wait until you're settled."

David trusted Ashley knew what was best for her son, but did she know what was best for herself?

At some point, she needed to settle down. Trent was crazy about Cory, and on more than one occasion had mentioned it would be good if Ashley stuck around this time. Apparently, the two siblings weren't on the same page.

"True. I need the extra time to figure things out." Ashley nodded, letting out a deep breath.

They returned to the kitchen, and David put pizza on a couple of plates while Ashley poured a glass of milk for Cory.

"Is sweet tea okay," she asked, holding up the jug.

"Yes, thank you. Doesn't your ex-husband have any say in where you move? I'm sure he misses Cory." David knew he was crossing into seriously personal information, but Ashley's situation with her ex baffled him, and he was hoping to find out more. Trent was worried about her. And if Trent was concerned, so was David. And then some.

"Probably not." Ashley glanced at her son as if to verify he wasn't listening.

"That's odd. I couldn't imagine not missing a kid like Cory. A bundle of joy in a four-year-old body." David laughed.

"I agree, but then Joe and I are two different people. Which is why we're divorced." Ashley shrugged.

She surprised him by even answering, but her answer sounded all wrong. David decided to press for more. "I take it the divorce wasn't amicable?"

Ashley's eyes darkened, a quick indicator he'd gone too far. "I'd rather not talk about my personal life. I think we should stick to the festival plans." She delivered the milk to Cory and returned to the table to sit opposite him.

Her refusal to discuss the matter concerned him. He cared about Ashley, and if Joe Stanton had done anything to hurt her or Cory, the man would have plenty to answer for, and not just to Trent.

"Do you have the list?" he asked, taking the hint to change the subject.

"I do. It's right here." She reached into her purse, pulled out the paper she'd stuffed there earlier, and slid it in his direction.

David glanced over their assigned projects. "It says here we have to make three signs and based on the details provided and then hang them at the designated spots. And there's a box of five hundred flyers we need to pick up at Sally's. We are supposed to hang them around town, in Glen Haven, and on the road to Lancaster. We also have three craft booths to erect. This is quite a list, and there's not much time to get it done, considering we are both busy." Not to mention, there were only two of them until Trent returned.

"Trent should be here in a couple of days." It was as if she'd read his mind. "Maybe if we get the signs made and hung, and work on putting up the flyers, we can wait for him to work on the booths. The extra set of hands will come in handy."

"Again, that's a lot to do in a short amount of time. Are you willing to put in a few hours working with me every day? And what about Cory?"

"It's not like we have a choice. We both agreed. We can meet at three p.m. the next couple of days to work on the flyers and signs. It'll be something Cory can do with us."

David couldn't help but wonder if Cory was her insurance against him getting overly personal or of it was merely a convenience. Probably both. "I guess that will work. I'll even bring Kojak to help keep Cory in line," he added, trying to get on board with the plan.

"Great. And I'll update Trent unless you talk to him first."

"Sounds good. And Cory can help with the art-work on the signs."

"He'd love that. And then if anyone comments on our lack of artistic ability, we can say Cory did it." Ashley grinned. The smile tugged at the corners of his heart, reminding him of the numerous times he'd kissed that sweet smile.

"That's a great idea." David chuckled.

An awkward silence fell between them, Ashley fidgeting with the napkin in front of her. "I've got—"

"I should probably—" David started to speak at the same time. "Go ahead, ladies first."

Ashley shot him a tentative smile. "Thanks. I need to talk to you about something. We have a problem, and I'm hoping you and I can work it out peacefully." Her words and tone didn't bode well.

David gazed back at her, giving her his undivided attention.

"Well, you already know that I'm searching for the bald eagle or a nest for the Audubon Society." Ashley shredded the napkin as David waited for the bomb to drop.

She was definitely up to something or wanted something. If it concerned the eagle and her earlier pleas to postpone the burn, she would be sorely disappointed. "Yes. Did you find the eagle?" It would change everything if she had, but he didn't think that was the case, or it would have been the first thing out of her mouth at the committee meeting today when she saw him.

"No, I haven't seen the eagle. But I do think I might have heard it today out by one of the ponds." Ashley looked at Cory as he played with Kojak. Avoiding his gaze more than likely.

"Were you planning on going back out there tomorrow?" David asked, knowing the burn was due to proceed bright and early in the a.m., and she wouldn't be allowed anywhere near the area.

"I was planning on it. The thing is, when I was out there, I came across something." Ashley reached into her camera bag and pulled out a red flag with a logo emblazoned across it. The White Mountain Fire District logo.

"Where did you get that?" he asked, knowing the answer, but praying he was wrong.

"I came across it today while I was out searching one of the gridded sections on my map. In fact, there were a lot of them in a row. There was a twenty-foot-wide path cleared where they were located. Is it safe for me to assume that this is the line of your controlled burn?" Her eyes fixated on him as she revealed the crux of the conversation.

"Yes. The wide path is dug to give us protection to keep the burn from jumping the line to unintended areas." He knew Ashley wouldn't let this go, and unfortunately, they were on opposite sides of an issue. "Can you show me where you found the flag?"

Ashley pulled the map from her briefcase and opened it wide across the table. She took her pencil and drew a circle around one of the grids. "This is where I was today, and the dotted line indicates where I found the flags and the direction they ran."

"That's the southern parameter of the prescribed burn. We're scheduled to start in that area tomorrow and move north. You won't be allowed back anywhere near there until we're finished."

"Tomorrow? Based on what you said, I thought I had more time. You can't go in there and burn, not while there's a chance the eagle is there. What if there's a nest? Or immatures still using the nest? Please, can't you stall the burn another week?" she pleaded.

"Ashley, I have to do my job. We don't know there's an eagle there. We moved up the burn because the weather conditions changed, and we need to take advantage. If we wait, the conditions could change, and we'll have missed our last window of opportunity until later this fall."

"But what about the bald eagle? Surely he has a right to federal protection if he's living here." Her voice bordered on desperation making him wonder what else was going on in her head.

"We both know a bald eagle's territory can be roughly a couple of miles in all directions from where spotted. We also know he could have been passing through, if, in fact, the reported sighting is even accurate. That's a lot of what-ifs and hypotheticals. We have a fire department to run. I know it's not what you want to hear, but it's reality. These controlled burns protect the forest, the people that live in this area, our communities, and even the wildlife. We can't put all that on hold for a suspected bald eagle sighting. I'm all for what you're doing, but you can't ask the fire department to stop a process that's taken months to put in place, and that helps the greater good."

Ashley sat back, her arms crossed in defiance. Clearly, it didn't matter what he said, she would only see it her way.

"You're the battalion chief, and you can do anything you want. Consider it a favor for me, please," she begged. Her eyes filled with the tears, making it all that much harder not to give in to her impassioned plea.

"Battalion chief is third in command. I've got two other bosses ahead of me, including the fire chief, that say I can't cancel it without a better reason than a suspected eagle sighting. And even if I was in Chief Anderson's position, honestly, I'd have to look at the big picture. I'm sorry that's not what you want to hear."

Ashley stood and walked away, brushing at her tears with her sleeve. She turned back to him. "It always has to be your way, doesn't it? The eagles are important, David, but they're not the only reason. If I find a new pair of eagles nesting in the area, the coverage might just be what I need to make the job with National Geographic a shoe-in. I need this for Cory's and my future." He knew there had been more to her impassioned pleas for his help, but it didn't change his answer.

"That's not a fair statement given the situation. Give me proof, and I'll stop the burn. It's that easy." David stood, realizing the evening had come to a crashing halt. So much for getting along and working together.

"I don't have proof, and you know it. Only the reported sighting. The people were registered birders with a good track history. But I feel it in my heart, that he's out there somewhere. I can't explain it, just that I believe it."

David started for the door. "I can't change what's scheduled based on a feeling, and you know it." Kojak spotted him and ran to his side.

Ashley grabbed his arm to keep him from leaving. "What can I do to make you stop this?"

"Short of finding the eagle, getting an injunction, or having an in with Mother Nature to make the conditions unfavorable, there isn't anything you can do to change the outcome tomorrow."

Ashley dropped her hand. "Then I guess I have to find the eagle."

"Unfortunately, you won't have the chance in that designated area. We'll be blocking it off first thing in the morning, and no one will be allowed near the area as a safety precaution."

Ashley shook her head. "This is all wrong."

"My hands are tied. I'll meet you at Sally's tomorrow at three to hang the flyers. If anything comes up with the burn that's going to make me late, I'll text you."

"I'm not sure I want to work with you on the festival," Ashley shot back at him.

"That's up to you. There's a lot to be done, and the people in the community are counting on everyone to pitch in and do their part. Surely you can put aside our differences and do what you promised to do." He was goading her into sticking with the plan, mostly because he'd looked forward to spending time with her. But also, because he didn't want things to remain tense between them, He much preferred the easy camaraderie they'd shared tonight over pizza.

"Fine. Three o'clock. Doesn't mean I have to like it." Ashley's voice rippled with displeasure. So, she'd be there, but it wouldn't change the tension or her dislike. That part was out of his hands.

"Excellent. See you there. Good night, Cory."

"Good night, Mr. David. Thanks for bringing Kojak and pizza. He's a great dog and my new best friend. Just like my bunny Jax." David wished Ashley felt the same way about him. He turned back to her, hoping there was something he could say or do to make things better.

"I've got it," Ashley cried out, a sudden smile lighting her face.

"What's that?" he was almost afraid to ask.

"I can't control Mother Nature, and I don't have time to find the eagle, but...I can go for the injunction you mentioned. It was a great idea. Thank you."

David winced. This was a twist he hadn't expected. He'd been teasing when he suggested it but leave it to Ashley to seize the idea.

Chief Anderson wouldn't be pleased with the turn of events, and it would only bring negative attention to the fire department within the community. When the people of Hallbrook got wind of her righteous cause, they'd forget all about why David was doing the controlled burn in the first place. There was only one thing on his side that might help stop Ashley.

There wasn't enough time for her to get an injunction before the burn, even if she could find a judge willing to listen.

# Chapter Seven

♥

ASHLEY DIALED THE NUMBER for the sheriff's office the second the door closed behind David. She needed to find out what it would take to get an injunction to stop David and the White Mountain Fire Department from doing the controlled burn. And all by morning. It was the perfect solution, and she had David to thank for it, although he probably didn't see it that way. But then it didn't matter what he thought—her job was to stop him.

"Hallbrook Sheriff's Department, this is Lieutenant Adams. Is this an emergency?"

*Sort of.* "Yes and no. My name is Ashley Stanton, and I'm part of the Bald Eagle Project for the state. I was searching for a nest today and came across the White Mountain Fire Department flags where they intend to start a controlled burn in the morning."

"Yes, ma'am. I'm familiar with their plan, and I've heard about your eagle efforts. The town is really hoping you'll be successful."

"Well, the problem is the burn runs the risk of running off the eagle and destroying the nest if there's a mated pair. And if there's an immature in the nest, there's no telling what could happen. What can I do to get an injunction to stop them and give me more time to locate the bald eagle or a nest?" Ashley stopped pacing; her eyes closed as she prayed, hoping he'd have the answer she needed to hear.

"Well, ma'am, the judge has already gone home for the day, and I'm not sure there's much we can do. I mean, have you spotted a bald eagle?"

"I have not, but I'm almost positive he's near here based on the sighting and the timing of the report."

"I'm sorry, Ms. Stanton, almost positive is not enough to stop the fire department from doing their job."

"The bald eagle is federally protected. You have to help me," she begged.

"Ma'am, I realize the bald eagle is federally protected. Trust me, the best I can tell you to do is to go over to the courthouse in the morning and apply for an injunction. Unfortunately, by then, the burn will have already started. But you might shut them down early if the judge agrees with you."

The man seemed genuinely sorry, and it wasn't his fault things weren't working out the way she wanted. Ashley thanked him and hung up the phone, her spirits deflated. She'd hoped tossing around the word bald eagle would help. Clearly, she'd thought wrong.

"Cory, honey. You need to put your pajamas on. We've got an early day tomorrow, and you're going to Tricia's again."

"Yippee! I really like it here, Mommy. When can I get a dog like Kojak?" It was the same question he'd asked hundreds of time before. And she hadn't expected anything different after he'd spent the evening playing with the friendly dalmatian.

She shook her head. "Someday, honey. Mommy's got to figure out a few more things, and we need to be more settled. The timing's just not good right now."

"You always say that," Cory answered, his lower lip dropping into a pout.

"Skedaddle. Bedtime. I'll be in shortly to make sure you brushed your teeth and to tuck you in. Don't forget to pick a bedtime story." She smiled as he wandered down the hall to do what he was told.

Ashley's phone rang, Trent's name flashing across the screen. She pressed the answer button, needing a friendly ear to pour out her troubles to.

"Hey, sis. Just thought I should check in on my favorite sister and see how things are going?"

"I'm your only sister, wise guy. And I've had the worst day." She let out a deep sigh. All her efforts to find the eagle had been a complete failure. She wasn't naïve enough to believe the eagle would stick around with a fire nearby. It's not like they would understand what was happening to their home.

"Don't tell me you burned down David's place, too?" Trent laughed.

"Hardly." Trent didn't understand, but his comment was a subtle reminder she needed to remember the blessings in her life as well as the hardship she was fixating on.

"Then what's going on? I was calling to let you know I'll be home on Tuesday. That is, unless you need me before then?"

Tuesday was too late to be of use to her, much the same way an injunction tomorrow would be too late. "What I need is someone with connections." She carried Cory's plate and glass to the kitchen, multitasking while she walked and talked.

"What kind of connections?" he asked, curiosity in his voice.

"The kind that can get a hold of the judge after hours."

Trent was silent on the other end of the phone for the space of at least five seconds. "I've got connections, and I might be able to get in touch with the judge, considering I'm dating his daughter. What's going on that you need to reach him after hours? Can't it wait till morning?"

"It's an emergency. The eagle I'm searching for could be in danger. The fire department starts the controlled burn in the morning, and it crosses into the area I'm looking. If the eagle is anywhere in the vicinity, he'll leave. And what if the nest is in the area they're burning? It could kill an immature eagle not ready to fly. We can't let them destroy the eagle's habitat." Ashley poured every ounce of emotion she had into her passionate plea for help. Trent was her last hope.

"By them, I take it you mean David?" Trent asked, zeroing in on the other problem with getting him to agree to help.

"Yes. He's in charge of the controlled burn, and he won't listen to me. Instead, he goes on and on about doing his job." It's not that she didn't understand his position, she did. But there had to be some wiggle room in between what they both wanted.

"Listen, Ashley, I'm not sure about this. Asking for a favor is one thing, but you're also asking me to step in between you and David, my best friend. That's putting me in a tough place."

"But I'm your sister. Your allegiance should be to me. I'm only asking for a few more days." More like a week, based on the territory she had yet to cover. But Trent didn't need to know the specifics.

"Tell you what I'll do." Trent let out a deep breath. "I'll call the judge and ask for a hearing. He won't grant the injunction without one. But if he grants you a hearing, it should give you a forty-eight hour temporary injunction. You'll both present your sides, and the judge will decide how to rule. David will be furious, but it's the only way I know to keep me out of the decision process."

Ashley's heart raced with renewed hope. "I love you. I love you. I love you. Thank you. You won't regret this, I promise." Not that she had any idea whether he would or not, because there was no way to know how this would all play out.

"Now you love me. I see how it is." Trent was back to his normal teasing. "But, Ashley, remember it could only buy you forty-eight hours. You need to find the eagle or have solid proof he exists. The judge won't budge on this one if you don't."

The reminder of the time constraint dampened her spirits considerably. But she'd make it work because she had the power of positive thinking on her side. Look how far it had gotten her tonight. "I'm on it. I'll be back out there first thing in the morning."

"Oh, and one other thing, Ashley. I'd prefer it if you didn't tell David I'm the one who pulled this off for you. It would be better all the way around if I'm not involved."

"That's fine. Whatever you want works for me. I find it interesting though that you're close enough to the judge that you can just call him. I thought you said you and Maria weren't serious?"

"Well, actually, we are exclusive. And it is serious."

"Nice." Ashley was more than a little surprised. "Why didn't you tell me before?" She shook her head, hurt that he hadn't said anything. It's not like she'd unloaded on anyone about her divorce, so his assumption she was in a dark place stung. Far from it, truthfully. During the past week, she'd come to realize more and more it was for the best.

The truth was, she wasn't even sure she'd ever been in love with Joe. She'd loved the security and fun he offered, but real love? Time had proven they weren't suited. Something she would have figured out before she agreed to marry him if she'd paid closer attention.

"Goodnight, Trent. Make your call and let me know how it goes."

Forty-five minutes later, a text notification chirped on her phone.

*Trent: Mission Accomplished. Except thirty-six hours based on timing. Court hearing Friday 8 a.m.*

*Knock. Knock.*

David glanced at his watch. Nine p.m. was a little late for somebody to come knocking at his door. His first thought was he was needed at work, but they would have called.

*Ashley.*

*Woof.* Kojak let out a low-pitched bark, raising the alarm. The dog glanced first toward the front door and then at David, who quickly moved to answer the door, worried something was wrong. He was surprised to see Sheriff Haskins standing there but was relieved there was nothing wrong with Ashley.

"Evening, Wyatt. What brings you out my way? I would have thought you'd be home by now," David said, reaching out to shake hands.

"I would've been if it wasn't for your tenant," Wyatt grumbled.

"My tenant?"

"Ashley Stanton." Wyatt tapped the envelope he was holding against David's chest. "I don't know how she managed to pull this off, but that little lady put a stop to the controlled burn tomorrow." Wyatt shook his head.

"What do you mean?" David frowned, taking the envelope, but unsure what to think. He pulled the envelope open and slid out the document.

"It's a temporary injunction. She managed to buy herself thirty-six hours before you two have a court date Friday morning. You get to face off with Ms. Stanton, and the judge will make a ruling on whether to extend the injunction on the burn for another week. Sorry, but I had to deliver the news once I got the call." Wyatt removed his hat and ran a hand through his hair.

"You've got to be kidding me. We've been planning this for close to a month, and Ashley can put a halt to it within hours? Two days may be too late, a week is out of the question. We'd be smack dab in the July 4th festivities."

"Little lady must have some friends in high places, I reckon. At least he didn't give her the standard forty-eight. That would have pushed it to Monday morning."

*Trent.* It wasn't exactly a secret his best friend was dating the judge's daughter. And as angry as he was at Trent for doing this, he also realized Ashley was his friend's sister. A person that also deserved his allegiance. Trent had been caught between the two of them, something that shouldn't have happened in the first place.

"This is ridiculous, but I'll Chief Anderson and let him and everyone else know that the burn is off tomorrow. Let's just hope the weather cooperates and we can do it right after the hearing."

"Have a good night, David. I've got to get home to the wife." Wyatt stepped out the door and onto the front porch.

"Send her my apologies for you being late." David waved as the man got in his patrol car and backed out of the driveway.

He looked down at the paper he held in his hand. A temporary injunction. The only reason Ashley even knew something like that would work was that he'd opened his big mouth about it. David hoped it wouldn't mean they couldn't complete the burn until fall because the idea of a wildfire in summer was a firefighter's worse nightmare.

An out-of-control fire wouldn't save her eagle, either. David cared about the forest and the animals that lived in them. But he also cared about the people in the community. It was a hard job balancing both. But seeing as Ashley had found a way to get around him for two days, he'd say she won this round. But unless she came up with a bald eagle between now and the court hearing, nothing would change.

David pressed the speed dial for his boss, not looking forward to the call at all. "Hey, Chief. I just got served with temporary injunction papers stopping the burn tomorrow. I'll alert the guys on duty tonight and send messages to everyone, so they know the change in plans."

"What happened?" Chief Anderson demanded. "What's going on? We've had this thing planned for a while, and the weather's finally right. If we miss this, we could be done for the season." Nothing David hadn't already thought about.

"A woman by the name of Ashley Stanton is what happened. She's working with the Audubon Society in search of a bald eagle or a nest to establish the accuracy of a reported sighting. Apparently, her search area connects with our burn area. She hasn't found anything yet, and this is just a stall tactic. Unfortunately, we do have to play by their rules."

"A bald eagle, huh? It'd be great if we had one. But do you know how many times somebody sees an osprey and claims they saw an eagle?"

"I have a pretty good guess the number is high." David was positive it was true.

"I don't like it when something like this gets in the way of us doing our job. Not to mention, if the people of Hallbrook and the surrounding towns find out what she's up to, they're liable to rally on her side. We don't need the locals pitted against the fire department. We've worked hard to maintain good relations with the community. You need to see what you can do to smooth things over. Talk to this woman."

"Trust me, I've talked to her," David said, knowing the chief wouldn't like his answer. And talking didn't matter now, not with the temporary injunction in hand.

"What's that supposed to mean?" Chief Anderson fired back.

"Ashley grew up right here in Hallbrook. Moved to California right after high school. She's Trent

Anderson's sister. Not to mention, for full disclosure, I used to date her in high school. Things didn't work out. And...she's also living in the apartment above my garage as of right now."

"What? Are we mixing business and pleasure?" Chief Anderson asked, authoritative concern in his voice. The man ruled by the book and expected others to do the same.

"Absolutely not, sir. She was burned out of the house she was renting, and I offered her a place to stay. My mother's currently not using her apartment. Nothing more than a favor for my best friend's sister." David knew it wasn't true, but the chief wouldn't want the truth.

Ashley Anderson was still very much deep in his heart, and he'd offered the place to stay because the opportunity to have her close had been a temptation too great to pass up.

"See that it stays that way," Chief Anderson ordered.

"Yes, sir." *If only it were that easy.*

# Chapter Eight

♥

ASHLEY DROPPED CORY OFF at Tricia's house bright and early, trying to get a jump start on the eagle search. She really needed to cancel her meeting with David this afternoon at the community center. Except she didn't dare, considering she'd already put a kink in one of his plans. It's not like she was here to make his life miserable. She was just doing what needed to be done, and that meant honoring her commitments—even if they were at odds with his.

When she arrived at the South Summit parking lot, she breathed a sigh of relief when there was no sign of David or the fire department. She quickly went to work, hoping to get through another section. By three p.m. she'd seen a fox, two rabbits, six deer, and umpteen songbirds, but no eagle.

There were only eleven more gridded sections left to check that centered around the reported sighting. Eagles could cover significant distances, but if Ashley didn't turn up any evidence soon, it wouldn't matter.

So far, David hadn't bothered to call. Ashley couldn't decide if that was a good or bad thing. He was probably more than a little ticked at her. She was late arriving to their meeting, but she half expected him to be a no-show. Pulling into the parking lot, she quickly realized the error of her thinking when she spotted his black truck. She slid out of her car, only to discover he'd already spotted her and made his way over to where she parked.

"I was wondering if you'd have the courage to turn up today," David said, getting straight to the point. No hello, or how do you do or anything. Honestly, she hadn't expected anything else.

"Me? Courage? Why would I not show up?" Ashley bristled at his implication, even if she had considered doing the no-show act. But it wouldn't have been for the reasons he suspected. She had eagle work to do and a time limit unless the judge extended the temporary injunction.

"Perhaps a sense of guilt for sabotaging the controlled burn this morning?" David shrugged.

"Oh, that. I just did what I had to do. I have no remorse. It's not like I got it canceled. Yet. The judge will decide that tomorrow morning." Ashley grabbed her backpack and lifted the straps over her shoulder. "I picked up the flyers from Sally's," she said, handing him one of the boxes. "We can each take a box and work separately." Together, yet apart.

"All you've done is stall the inevitable. You've got nothing, and we both know it. And finding a bald eagle in the White Mountain National Forest is like looking for an American Beetle. Odds are against you. Admit it." David drilled her with an intense gaze, willing her to tell the truth.

She'd always been honest with him and couldn't find it in her heart to be anything but truthful. "Okay, fine. I admit it. But it doesn't change anything."

His left eyebrow rose a notch, causing her to grin. "It's nice to see we can agree. I told you I would abide by the rules. So now the burn waits until Saturday." David's matter-of-fact response surprised her.

Maturity sat well with him. Not that he'd ever been immature, not that she could remember. At least, not since his father died. It was just that she hadn't expected him to be so obliging. "Just for the record, I'm not an entomologist, so I have no idea what you meant."

"Neither am I. I only knew the reference because it's something I picked up in one of my forestry classes. The American Beetle is endangered and harder to find than a bald eagle." David grinned.

"So, you're okay with this?" She nodded toward the flyers. "Working together?"

"Absolutely. We're both adults here last time I checked," David teased.

"I've noticed. But we were both adults the last time you walked away, so my experience with you isn't good."

His teasing smile vanished. "Ashley, I thought we agreed not to go down that road."

It hadn't been a nice thing to say considering how generous he'd been to her, but deep down, she still hurt. Which was a problem because it meant she

still cared. She'd crossed into the forbidden territory, but for the life of her, she couldn't stop the next
question. A question she'd waited over eleven years
to ask.

"You never explained why you broke it off with
me. Maybe I'd like the same closure you seem to
have. Maybe, after all these years, I want to know
what changed your mind. It's not like I had a real
explanation back then. No discussion. Nothing."
Tears welled her in her eyes, making him appear
blurry. She brushed them away furiously, hating for
him to see her weakness.

"Knowing wouldn't have changed anything. It
was better for you to hate me. I thought it would
make it easier for you to move on. And you did.
You're an amazing photographer with a wonderful
son. All things that might not have happened if
we'd stayed together." David stepped closer, one
hand coming up to cup her cheek softly. "What's
important for you to know is that I really did care
about you. I cared enough to do what I thought was
right all those years ago." His thumb brushed away
a fresh set of tears that trickled down her face.

"You're right. I'm just an emotional mess over the eagle. Sorry," Ashley said, pulling away from him, needing to end the moment. Better to put on her brave face. David was an expert at non-answers, and she knew now more than she knew back in high school. But there was no way she was buying into the fact he'd done it for her. No, he'd done what he wanted to do.

David turned and walked back to his truck, opening the door to let Kojak out.

Finally, something else to talk about. "Do you take the dog everywhere?" Ashley asked when he returned.

"Just about. Kojak's not much into stapling and hanging, but he's good for entertainment." David smiled, probably just as eager as she was to find common ground that didn't test emotional limits.

"I guess that means we're walking the streets to hang the signs?" It would be the better option to accomplish their goal, rather than hopping in and out of the car. The only problem was the long hike she'd already taken today and for the past several days. Her sore muscles were starting to catch up with her, not that she'd complain to David.

"You got it. It's not like Hallbrook is that big. And when we finish here, we can head over to Glen Haven and do the same thing."

Ashley groaned. "That's fine. I'm sure you've got it under control." And for once, she didn't mind.

They started down one side of Main Street, Ashley careful to keep an eye on the cracks that jumped up out of nowhere on the sidewalk. And then there was the occasional pedestrian out for a walk or shopping she tried to avoid bumping into. From lightpost to alternating lightpost, they moved down the street at a good clip, each doing their own thing. It gave Ashley plenty of time to think and remember far too much of the past.

The Sweeter Side of Life bakery was still open, and Ashley would have loved to stop. The idea of a warm pastry was more than a little appealing since she hadn't eaten enough to counter the today's calorie burn based on all the steps she'd taken. If she'd worn her step counter, they would have sent her a new achievement award.

A few people said hello to her, but for David, it was an all-out social fest. People honked and waved, called out from across the street, some stopped to talk, others to pet Kojak. Downtown Hallbrook was like Grand Central station when it came to Chief Beckett.

A petite and attractive woman approached David, her smile and hug indicative of the closeness between the two. Ashley couldn't help but hang back, trying to get a sense of the relationship between the two. Dressed in jeans and a blouse, the woman's coppery-red hair was pulled into a bun revealing oversized dangly silver hoop earrings. Topped off with perfectly applied makeup, and the woman exuded confidence in both looks and attitude.

"David, it's great to see you," the woman gushed. "And here's my big boy." She reached down and patted Kojak affectionately. "When are you going to come over and provide stud services? Lulu's ready again, and I can't wait. You promised, remember?"

Ashley coughed. This was a conversation she'd didn't want to hear. *At all.* She moved away, determined to miss his response. David Beckett was not the man she thought. Perhaps it was a good thing that things hadn't worked out between them.

She passed the Peterson's ice cream shop, the place known for the best ice cream in the county.

Memories of hours hanging out there with David assailed her, and Ashley shoved them away.

A breeze started to pick up, blowing her hair in her face. She brushed it back with one hand so she could see what she was doing, leaning her head to one side to help keep it that way. She set the box down and tried to hold the flyer in place as she stapled, but the breeze made the effort more difficult.

"Here, let me help," David said, coming to stand behind her and taking the flyer from her hands.

Ashley tensed. "I can do it," she said, trying to take the paper from him.

"Why don't I hold it in place, and you staple. Just please, avoid the fingers and thumbs. I don't relish the idea of leaving one of them hanging on a light pole," he teased.

Ashley wanted to wipe the grin right off his face. She brushed her hair behind her shoulder again. "I wouldn't do it on purpose if that's what you're suggesting." She looked up at him with raised eyebrows, sending the real message, that of course, she'd love nothing more than to do just that.

"What's wrong?" David asked, stepping back. "I was teasing."

"Are you and Miss Fancy Pants getting to-gether soon? I wouldn't want to interfere in your...*ummm*...private life." Ashley hated that she'd even verbalized the comment, but part of her need-ed to know.

"Maxine? What?" A sudden light dawned in his warm brown eyes, and his grin grew maddeningly wider. "I promised her Kojak for *stud* services. Lulu is her dalmatian." David shook his head, laughing.

How was she supposed to know? Okay, so maybe she shouldn't have jumped to conclusions, but she had. Better to make the best of a bad situation and move on. "Oh, I see. That's nice. We better get hanging these before the wind picks up anymore."

Judging by her reaction to Maxine, Ashley was in over her head. And now, standing pressed against David's back, her brain was turning to mush. Her breath hitched as she had to lean in close, trying to work around his shoulder to get close enough to the flyer to staple it to the pole without stapling his hand.

"This works much better." He turned his face toward her, bringing them cheek to cheek. *Kissing close.*

Ashley froze, allowing herself to remember, willing him to kiss her. A car honked, snapping her out of the forbidden zone she'd entered. "Yes, it will work better. Maybe we can get through this faster, and I can get back to Cory. I've been gone all day." It was a close save. If the car's horn hadn't interrupted, Ashley was afraid she might have made the first move and stolen the kiss anyway.

One of the flyers flew off the top of the pile and down the sidewalk. Kojak chased after it, barking. *Woof. Woof.* The dog proudly announced he'd captured the runaway paper, holding it in place with his paw. They both laughed, and David moved forward to retrieve the flyer and his dog.

Ashley shook her head, watching the two of them together. Man and his dog. David scratched Kojak behind the ears and dropped a kiss on his head. The two of them were close, best friends close.

David and Ashley made their way through town, hanging up the flyers together, only stopping at Sally's for a soda before heading to Glen Haven.

They spent the next hour and a half finishing the task, including hanging some of the flyers on the main road headed toward Lancaster.

"I'm glad that's done," Ashley said when they'd hung the last of the flyers.

"Me, too. You want to get some dinner?" David asked as they climbed back in his truck.

A flush of warmth rippled down her spine, leaving her giddy with excitement that he'd asked. A date? Her brain was clearly in overload mode. "Thanks, but no. I need to get back to Cory. And without the festival flyers to keep our conversation going, I worry we'll drift into a discussion about tomorrow morning, which I'm positive will not end well between you and me."

"It's just an injunction hearing. Whatever the judge rules will be fine by me." David shrugged, reinforcing his words.

"Seriously?" How could she believe him when he was fighting her in court?

"I'll do whatever I need to do. It's my job, I keep telling you that. This isn't personal, not for me anyway. I'm sure we can find things to talk about without crossing any forbidden lines." He chuckled.

Ashley was tempted to say yes. It's not like she was staying in town for long or would let herself fall in love with David again. Not that she'd necessarily ever fallen out, but well, she knew what she meant. She wasn't going down that road a second time. "Fine. Then I agree. Let me pick up Cory from Tricia's, and we can meet at O'Malley's. Give me about half an hour. Tops."

"That doesn't make any sense. We live at the same address, in case you've forgotten. Let's drop off your car, and we can pick up Cory and go to dinner together. There's plenty of room for his car seat."

It was unlikely she'd be forgetting they practically lived with each other. "But that would seem date like, and I'm positive that's not such a good idea." She looked at David, almost hoping he'd contradict her. She was a love-sick fool, or at the very least, turning into one again. As long as David didn't realize it, she'd be okay.

"It's not a date. It's two friends going out to eat." *So much for a contradiction.*

"So, we're just friends?" Ashley asked, wanting to confirm his words.

"Absolutely. I wouldn't have it any other way." David took her arm and led her back to the truck.

And neither would Ashley. That had been the hardest part of everything. On top of losing the man she loved, she'd lost her best friend. Not having him in her life had left her empty and alone, especially after her mother died. California had been her chance to break free and start over. Leave the past behind.

And here she was, smack dab in the middle of her past. But not for long. A job would come along, and she'd pick up her feet and move on again.

*Just her and Cory.*

# Chapter Nine

♥

DAVID MIGHT HAVE CONSORTED with the enemy last night, but it was difficult to think of Ashley that way. The evening had been friendly and fun, almost like old times, except for Cory. The kid was adorable, and it was hard for David not to think he could have been his son if he'd stayed with Ashley.

This morning was a different story. Today, they were due in court.

Dressed in his regulation uniform and armed for battle, he was ready to present the fire department's case to the judge. It wasn't often he found the occasion to wear the full uniform, preferring to stay more business casual amongst his peers. It helped that he was approachable when issues arose. It was all part of the community image the department tried to maintain.

Ashley's car was already gone when he left the house, which didn't surprise him, given her penchant for organization and promptness. Last night's truce ended as they said goodnight, Ashley's rejection of his offer to ride together more than proof.

David parked in front of the courthouse and spotted Ashley's car a few spaces farther down the street, confirming she was already way ahead of him. He walked up the steps and made his way through the metal detectors and security checkpoint.

"Good morning, Bert. How's the missus?" The middle-aged man worked full-time for the town and part-time as a volunteer at the fire department.

"She's doing better. Dr. Duncan said it's the flu. I'm staying far, far away." Bert grinned.

"Good idea. Which courtroom is the judge using today?"

"2B. I checked the docket and saw the hearing for the injunction was today. The whole town is talking about it."

"It's not a big deal. The judge will make a ruling, and that's the end of it."

"The town doesn't agree if you know what I mean," Bert said, handing him back his personal belongings.

David didn't know, but he was more than curious. Too curious not to ask. "What do you mean?"

"There's talk about you and Ms. Stanton. There's even a betting pool on whether the two of you will get back together."

David shook his head. Such was life in a small town. "Which way did you bet?" There wasn't any doubt in his mind Bert was in the pool.

He had the good graces to look embarrassed. "I'm on the wedding-bells side," he admitted sheepishly.

"Hope you didn't bet much because you'll lose. Ms. Stanton's leaving town, and I'm not on the market. Never have been, never will be. You should have asked me first." It was David's turn to grin as he walked away. Courtroom 2B waited.

Worn wooden planks formed the long corridor, echoing each step he took. The walls were lined with pictures of Hallbrook, dating back to the town's incorporation and documenting the rich history over the past hundred plus years.

David entered the courtroom, his gaze landing on Ashley seated in the third row, Cory next to her. The little boy spun around and caught sight of him, waving as David moved down the aisle to sit next to him. Ashley glanced up, but remained silent, only nodding by way of acknowledgement to his arrival. She was in full defense mode.

"Hi, Mr. David. My mom is going to court to beat a bad guy. What are you doing here?" *Out of the mouths of babes.*

"The bad guy?" He frowned, glancing at Ashley. He hadn't expected that from her.

She shrugged. "I didn't call you a bad guy. I told him I was trying to stop the people who wanted to burn the forest."

"Put like that, it's not a big leap." It bothered him more than he cared to admit that she'd put him in a bad light with Cory.

"Are you going to help beat the bad guy, Mr. David?" Cory asked, looking up at him for confirmation.

"No, I'm not. Apparently, I'm the bad guy." David winked at Cory, hoping to lighten the impact of the biased view Ashley had presented to the four-year-old.

Cory's face scrunched up in confusion. "You're going to burn the forest? I thought you put out forest fires. Like Smokey the Bear."

"I do. But occasionally, the fire department has to do what we call a controlled burn. It helps to keep the forest, the animals, and the people safe from wildfires that can get out of control."

"I know what out of control is. Mom said that to me one time when I was racing through the house and wouldn't stop. She didn't like it."

"Exactly. Your mom corrected you and made you stop to protect you from yourself." He shot Ashley a glance, catching the firm set of her jaw. At least she wasn't interrupting and was letting him explain to Cory. The kid might be too young to understand, but it was important he looked up to firefighters. Thinking they were the bad guy was bound to leave a lasting negative opinion. "It's the same thing in the forest. The burning I'm doing is good burning, in order to protect something bad from happening. When you get older, you will understand."

Cory looked back and forth between Ashley and him. "Why doesn't my mommy want you to burn then?"

"She's trying to protect the eagle she's looking for but can't find."

"Just because I can't find one, doesn't mean it's not there." To her credit, she'd remained silent through the whole interchange, at least until now.

"Tell it to the judge." David winked. He was trying to keep it light between them. No matter what the judge decided, they still had to work together on the festival setup, and they would still be friends. Or at least, he hoped so.

Ashley shook her head, a faint smile catching the corners of her mouth. "At least it doesn't look like we'll have to wait long, there's no one else here."

"Hallbrook is a small town, and our crime rate is pretty low. It's a good place to live and raise children." He meant every word.

She let out a deep sigh. "I remember."

"Then why are you so determined to leave?" Getting Ashley to consider staying might be foolhardy, but then he was a fool. For her.

"The place has more memories than I like." The words came out barely above a whisper.

"They're not all bad memories. I remember several really great ones." He remembered more than several. The only bad one between them was the day he'd walked away.

Ashley rolled her eyes. "I guess we see things differently."

The judge entered the chamber, and the bailiff raised his hand for quiet.

"All rise. The Honorable Judge Erwin will be presiding over the courtroom today," the bailiff said.

The judge moved into the room and sat at the oversized desk. He rifled through the files in front of him before nodding to the bailiff.

"We'd like to call Ms. Ashley Stanton to the witness stand."

Ashley leaned in toward Cory. "Stay here, and don't say a word, honey. Mommy will be right up at the front of the room," she whispered.

"Don't worry, I'll be right here with him." Their gazes locked for a brief second. Words were not necessary. They were on opposite sides of the court hearing, but they were on the same side when it came to her son.

Ashley nodded before moving to the front of the room, her steps slow. She raised her right hand as the bailiff swore her in, and then she sat facing the courtroom, avoiding David's gaze entirely.

The judge cleared his throat. "Ms. Stanton, this is an informal injunction hearing. Please present your case, keeping strictly to the facts for brevity. After you've finished, Chief David Beckett will be allowed to represent the fire department and present his case. There will be no cross-examination, and my decision will be final regarding the injunction. Is this understood?"

The judge's stern expression brooked no opposition. Friday mornings were normally the time the judge played golf, and he clearly didn't like having his routine disrupted.

"I understand, sir. And thank you for granting me this opportunity. At the end of May, the Audubon Society received a credible bird watcher report that a bald eagle was sighted not far from the South Summit trailhead that leads up to Mount Washington. Bald eagles tend to have a territory of up to two square miles. Based on the approximate place it was seen, there's a sixteen square mile potential territory range if the calculations permit the coverage in all possible directions from the estimated sighting coordinates.

"The Audubon Society asked me to search the area to see if I can find the bald eagle or a nest. I understand that although they're no longer on the endangered list, they are still federally protected. Not to mention, a bald eagle in this area would be the first. I've marked out the suspected territory in sixteen gridded sections, each representing one square mile, and using the coordinates of the first sighting as the center point.

"I've systematically been going through these gridded sections and have already covered five of them. On Wednesday, I came across the fire departments burn flags marking their eastern burn perimeter. The controlled-burn area crosses into the gridded sections I'm investigating." Ashley shifted in her seat, pausing for only a moment.

"I'm not asking to stop the burn completely unless, of course, I find the bald eagle or the nest. I'm only asking for more time before they do the burn.

The smoke alone could cause a pair of eagles to abandon their nest and their young. In a successful mating season, the eggs would have been laid somewhere between March and May in this area, and the fledglings ready to fly anytime now, but they would still be returning to their nest until they're ready to leave completely." Ashley turned pleading eyes back to David, willing him to understand.

"How long are you asking for?" the judge asked.

"Only a week. Ten days tops." She nodded. Doing one section per day and keeping up with Cory and the festival would be pushing it, and her imposition on Tricia, which is why she'd added the extra time. *Wiggle room.*

The judge's question made David think Trent's connections went deeper than he'd first imagined. Was it possible the judge would overrule the fire plan for a suspected bald eagle? He hadn't thought it likely, but now, he wasn't so sure.

"Is that all the information you want me to consider in my decision?" Judge Erwin asked.

"Yes, Your Honor," Ashley said, nodding.

"Thank you. You may step down." Ashley made her way back to where David and Cory were sitting.

"Chief David Beckett, please come forward to give your testimony," the judge ordered, not wasting any time to move this hearing forward.

David moved to the front of the room and was sworn in by the bailiff.

"You may proceed with the facts of your case," Judge Erwin said.

"Your Honor, thank you for taking the time to hear us both out. I represent the White Mountain Fire Department. As you know, my headquarters are here in Hallbrook. This controlled burn has been organized and planned out to the last detail for almost two months. Everything has been approved.

"Our objective is to have the burn completed prior to the July 4th festivities, a time when we see increased amounts of campers, hikers, and outdoor adventurists, which also means a higher risk of accidental fires. Our goal is to get in ahead of all that to reduce the chance of a disastrous wildfire. Mother Nature hasn't cooperated, and we've been waiting for the right conditions to proceed. We had them, but the temporary injunction caused us to put a halt to the prescribed burn.

"Time is running out, and if we miss this window of opportunity, it will be fall before conditions are right again. So while I understand Ashley Stanton's request, it's not in the best interest of the community to put this on hold. There is no evidence to support the idea that an eagle has nested here.

"Not even a single photograph. It's not uncommon for people to mistake ospreys and even vultures for eagles when they're soaring through the skies above. This could be a simple case of mistaken bird identity. Not enough for us to jeopardize the plan at this point."

Ashley jumped to her feet. "But I told you I'm almost positive I heard him. I'm not one of the inexperienced people you're referring to," she exclaimed, her face flushed red with emotion.

"Silence," the judge ordered. "You're out of line. I said there'd be no rebuttal." Judge Erwin ran his court with an iron fist, and Ashley's plea fell on deaf ears.

Ashley crossed her arms in front of her chest and cast her eyes downward, as if she were struggling to bite back a retort. "I'm sorry, Your Honor." She sat back down.

Satisfied, the judge turned back to him. "Would you like to add anything to your statement?" Judge Erwin asked.

"Only that Ms. Stanton did tell me that she thought she heard an eagle, but that doesn't change the fact she hasn't seen one."

The judge frowned, well aware of what David had just done. By repeating Ashley's statement under oath, the judge would be forced to include it in his decision. It's not as if he thought the information would change the outcome, but he wanted Ashley to know he cared about the cause. And her.

Ashley looked up at him, her grateful expression warming his heart. She knew exactly what he'd done, and it looked as though she appreciated it.

"In light of hearing both statements, I've made my decision. With no proof photographically or visually, I cannot agree to interfere with the White Mountain Fire Department's approved plan of action for the prescribed burn. Injunction denied." The judge hammered his gavel on the desk, stood, and left the room.

Ashley looked close to tears as she grabbed Cory's hand and pulled him toward the aisle, trying to escape the room, and most likely, him.

"Wait, Ashley. I'm sorry. I tried to prepare you for the inevitable. I know it's not what you wanted to hear, but we can't run life on emotions and feelings. Facts. Plans. Laws. Rules. You know the routine." David was trying to help her be reasonable about the outcome. He didn't want her taking the judge's decision out on him or their renewed friendship.

"What I know is that you have the power to help, and you won't," she snapped. Apparently, the friendship ship had sailed.

"I'm not the fire chief, and you know it. I have bosses to answer to, just like most people. Yes, I have some power, but I don't make the final decision. I'd have to have a pretty good reason to cancel the burn, and I'll be laughed right out of the office if I tell my boss it's because you suspect there's an eagle in the forest with zero proof." David was trying his best to make her see reason, but she was as far from reasonable right now as she could be. She was taking the defeat hard.

Her gaze grew shuttered. "Never mind. Do whatever it is you need to do. All the more reason for Cory and me to get out of Hallbrook. My work is done here if you're going ahead with the burn. For your sake, I hope there aren't eagles out there. Because in the event there are, they probably have a nest and fledglings. And if the burn drives away the parents, the fledglings left behind will die. That'll be on your conscience," she snapped.

Ashley pulled her son behind her as they headed for the big double doors. Cory had remained quiet, his expression one close to tears as he watched his mother and David argue.

David didn't want to be a failure in Cory's eyes. Or Ashley's for that matter. Not to mention, he owed her big time for the hurt he'd caused when they were younger. Maybe, just maybe, there was a way to compromise. Something that would let them both call this a win. "Ashley, wait. I have an idea."

She stopped, turning back, a hopeful expression on her face. "What's that?"

"A compromise of sorts. What if I push the southern perimeter line farther north, to the edge of your grid line?" David would have to convince the chief it was a good idea at the last minute. Still, it would go a long way to limit the negative publicity this could bring to the area. Life was about compromise, something he'd learned later in life. *Too late for him and Ashley.*

"You'd do that? Can you do that?" she asked, the excitement back in her eyes.

"I can try. I need to run it by the chief, but since it's not canceling the burn, only adjusting the perimeter. There's a possibility I might be able to convince him. If you show me on the map what you need, I'll take it to the chief. No promises, but I will try. For you."

Her answering smile warmed his heart. "I have a better idea. Will you be burning tomorrow?"

"No. That was something else I planned on telling you after the hearing. The humidity levels aren't ideal, and weather conditions are a critical part of the formula. We were going to have to hold up another day."

"Wow, I had no idea the criteria are that specific." Ashley nodded, the light in her eyes returning as she absorbed the meaning of his words.

"There's usually not more than a dozen days each year that will get approved as ideal."

"Well, in that case, it means I have another day to search. I'm going to take advantage of it. While I'm still searching, there's always hope." Her excitement was contagious, and David couldn't help but hope she would find the bald eagle.

"That there is." He smiled, relieved to see her back to her old self. Ready to kick butt and take on the world.

"I'm going to search for a little while today, but tomorrow, if you're not working, why don't you come with Cory and me? We can walk off the line together. You can help me search for the eagle. Maybe it will give you a better appreciation for what I'm doing." Ashley reached out to touch his arm, her request genuine.

"I already have an appreciation for what you're trying to do. But, yes, it sounds like a good idea." Spending time with Ashley had always been at the top of his list of things to do. That hadn't changed apparently, his quick acceptance proof.

"Not to mention, I'll have you to help carry Cory when he gets tired." She laughed, and the warm sound wrapped around his heart and squeezed.

"Nice to know I'm good for something."

# Chapter Ten

♥

ASHLEY COULDN'T ESCAPE THE rush of happiness coursing through her body, knowing David was about to enter her world. With her. They were sharing something unique and beautiful together. Like old times.

And even though she was still concerned that moving the burn line wasn't enough, it was a generous offer on his part, and one she'd gladly accepted. Cory had been begging to go with her, and she'd seized the opportunity to include him. Anything to keep her offer for David to join her aboveboard. And safe.

A knock on the front door alerted her of David's arrival. Ashley pulled it open, momentarily stunned by the handsome man dressed in jeans and a tight red faded T-shirt that revealed firm biceps. He was totally prepared for a trek through the woods, right down to his hiking boots and an Indiana Jones style hat. *Scrumptious.*

"Good morning. I wondered if you'd back out of our arrangement. Glad to know you're a man of your word."

"I am." David nodded, his steady gaze never leaving her face.

They were both aware that once upon a time, he'd broken his word. David had promised to take her to prom, but then suddenly, not only did he break off the date, but he also broke off their relationship. For good. No explanations. Just done.

But for once, Ashley didn't feel like calling him out on it. Maybe it was time to let go of the past. After all, she had Cory and wouldn't change that for anything in the world. And David still had no one. He led a lonely life, by the looks of things, other than taking care of his mother. Sure, he did things in the community, but what did David do for himself?

She was the first to look away, as Cory started tugging at her leg.

"I'm ready, Mommy. Good morning, Mr. David. Look, I tied my own shoes. And these are the big boy kind with strings and everything," Cory said, pointing at his sneakers.

"Good morning, Cory. You did a great job." David smiled, ruffling the hair on the top of her son's head.

"Very nice, Cory." She gave her son a hug.

David reached into the backpack he carried. "I've got a surprise for you, Cory." He handed him a folded brown paper bag.

"I like surprises." Cory beamed.

"I didn't have time to wrap it, but I'm hoping that's okay?" David winked at Ashley.

Cory pulled something red and white and silky out from the bag. He dropped the paper to the ground in order to check out his gift. "What is it?" he asked, holding up the material.

"It's an American superhero cape. The Velcro right here snugs it around your neck, keeping your hands free for superhero adventures." David smiled, taking the cape from Cory's hands and helping him to put it on.

"This is so cool. It looks like a flag. Can I wear it today?" He hugged David.

"I was hoping you would. You never know when we might need a superhero."

Cory ran around the room, testing out his abilities, laughing, and chatting the whole time.

"That was sweet of you." Ashley nodded. "I've got a backpack prepared with some drinks, snacks, and lunch."

"What can I do to help?"

"Your contribution is bringing yourself." She grinned, picking the backpack up off the table and handing it to him. "Here, hold this while I put on my hiking boots."

"Mommy said we're going on an adventure hike. Isn't that cool?" Cory asked, bubbling with excitement.

"What's an adventure hike?" David asked, playing innocent.

"It's when you go on a long walk but get to find lots of really cool things." Cory grinned, pleased to be an authority on adventure hikes.

"I like the sound of that." David chuckled.

Cory peered around David's legs, looking toward the still open front door. He scrunched his face up like a prune. "Where's Kojak? Mommy said you would bring him."

"He's already in the truck waiting on us. The woods are his favorite place to be, and its great exercise. He's got to stay in top health to be a fire dog," David explained.

Satisfied, Cory's smile was firmly back in place. "Him and I can be buddies. And you and Mommy can be buddies. You always need a buddy when you're out in the woods in case you get lost or attacked by a bear."

"That's a good motto. But if you don't bother the bears, they generally won't bother you." David glanced up, his grin a familiar sight. One that always preceded a teasing remark. "I'll stick close to your mommy's side to make sure she doesn't get lost."

"He's gonna make a great buddy for you, Mommy. Let's go," Cory said, grabbing his own small backpack, one he'd gotten for Christmas this past year. Packed inside were a pair of binoculars, a magnifying glass, a net, a compass, and a couple of small containers. Everything a little boy needed for an adventure hike.

Ashley opted not to answer her son's comment, feeling it was better left alone. "Hang on, let me grab my camera bag." She double-checked to make sure she had everything. "All right, then, let's go."

Kojak was waiting for them, his head hanging out the window, and his tongue hanging out of his mouth. Ashley shook her head and laughed.

Cory bounded forward, just as eager to see the dog, as he was to go on an adventure hike.

"Can I ride in the back seat with the dog?" Cory asked.

"Of course." Ashley moved Cory's car seat into the back row seating area. David came around from the other side and latched it in. He lifted Cory into the seat, helping him to get situated before buckling the straps and then testing them like a pro.

"Looks like you've done that a time or two," she said, quite impressed considering he didn't have children of his own.

"We give car-seat-safety training at the department. Same thing with helmet safety and a few other kid-friendly programs." David gently assisted her up into the passenger seat.

"Nice."

"We try to be." He winked before closing the door. Ashley watched as he came around the truck, continually amazed by his generosity and kindness. The man was a natural with kids and deserved a few of his own. Although the idea of him with another woman didn't sit well. It had been the only consolation to their breakup. He hadn't left her for another woman. And according to Trent, David had never dated anyone seriously over the past years.

His *I don't do forever* was genuine.

She opened the map to show him the area she planned to cover today. "Look. These are the areas I still need to check. We can head over to the South Summit entrance where there's a trail that will take us right to this one." Ashley tapped the gridded sections to emphasize her point.

"Sounds like a plan. But it's not just a matter of simply moving the lines. As soon as I see firsthand what the proposed change will do, I can make sure the lay of the land supports the move. It depends on ground contours, area brush, and trees, amongst other things. If it checks out, I'll call the guys to come back out and remark the area, provided the chief agrees. A prescribed burn is very scientific to ensure the safety of everyone involved, the wildlife, and the habitat. There's no room for mistakes." David was as impassioned about what he did as she was about the eagles. He believed in what he was doing and did it with all his heart.

"I get it. And I appreciate you doing this. I really do. I'm still concerned about the smoke, but at this point, every little bit will help. The last thing I want to do is call the Audubon Society and tell them to close the report before I've had a chance to finish checking the area. But we all know the eagles will abandon their nest if they feel threatened."

David shook his head. "Sounds a bit dramatic for an eagle you don't know is really here."

Ashley frowned. "We're going to have to agree to disagree on that point. He's here. Somewhere. Most likely," she added. It was a feeling she hadn't been able to shake, and she believed it now more than ever.

"I'll give you this, you sure are persistent." He grinned.

"In my line of work, I have to be. Sometimes it can take days, weeks, or even months to find exactly what I'm looking for when it comes to getting the right shot. Mother Nature and wildlife don't always cooperate with human schedules."

"Now that I completely understand."

Cory played happily with Kojak in the backseat, oblivious to the discussion upfront. It wasn't long before they pulled into the parking lot next to the trailhead.

Ashley helped Cory out of is car seat and David let Kojak jump out. The two of them raced to the trail, stopping to wait for the adults.

"I'll carry the backpack, and you can focus on the camera," David offered. "We can both keep an eye on Cory and Kojak, but just so you know, Kojak's probably been through these woods more times than I can count. He knows his way around." David shrugged into the backpack and adjusted the straps.

"That's good to know. I'm sure you know the area, too, Mr. Boy Scout. But as a safeguard, I always carry a compass. I've learned to trust them explicitly. Otherwise, I can't return to places I need to with any degree of precision. It comes in handy when you have a sighting."

"Girl scout meets boy scout. Sound like fun. Ladies first." David grinned, gesturing toward the trail.

Ashley led the way. Or she did when they first started. It didn't take long for Cory and Kojak to take the lead, running ahead and then stopping to check out things they found. The two of them made quite the pair. Ashley wouldn't let him get far, the dangers of him wandering off or the rare possibility of a wild animal always still a reality she couldn't ignore.

She pointed out several of the flowers, trees, and bushes, identifying them as they went. David knew a lot of them, but he appreciated learning about the ones he didn't.

They came to a rock outcropping, and David strategically used his hands and feet to get to the top. He then turned and gave a hand to Cory, pulling him up. Kojak barked, and then ran around the rock, searching for a way to get to the top.

David offered Ashley a hand. She accepted his help w without giving it a second thought, putting her foot on the ledge to push as he pulled. Except she pushed a little too hard, considering his pull, and landed smack dab in his arms, almost knocking them both off-balance.

"Whoa." She reached out to steady herself, her hands landing on his rock-solid chest.

"Are you falling for me?" he teased. Talk about boyish charm. The man had it in spades.

"Not a chance. That was your Popeye pull, more than anything I did." She stepped back, trying to recover her sanity.

"If you say so." David grinned, not believing a word of her accusation. "Kojak, stay," he ordered when the dog barked again, not liking to be left out of the fun.

They stood at the top of the rock outcropping, Ashley holding on to Cory's hand tightly. This wasn't the time for Cory to be the brave, independent type of child. Together, they all searched the skies, each hoping to be the one to spot an eagle. It was nice that David was here and helping. All the other times she'd searched, it hadn't been nearly this much fun. But this time, she had three male companions to make her feel special. What more could a girl ask for?

*To keep them all.*

"It's beautiful here," Ashley said, taking in the majestic mountains stretched out before them.

"It's one of my favorite viewpoints. I don't get out here often enough, so thanks."

"Your welcome. I'm really glad you came with me today."

"Me too," David said, turning to leave, and taking Cory with him.

Ashley took one last glance, scanning the skies from one end to the other of her view. Off in the distance, she spotted a couple of large birds flying. "Hold up, David. Look." she said, pointing toward the two birds soaring through the air, riding the current.

"Are they the eagles?" David asked, rejoining her.

"I'm not sure yet. The birds are too far away to tell." Ashley lifted her binoculars and adjusted the focus, zeroing in on the birds. "They're kettling like eagles, but honestly, I don't think it's them." *Another disappointment.*

"Kettling?" he asked.

"It's when they soar on the air currents. It's their favorite thing to do when the wind currents are right." Ashley let out a deep sigh. The V-shaped wing pattern indicated they were vultures.

"I thought a kettle was something you boiled water in," Cory said, making her and David laugh.

"Different type of kettle, I'm guessing," David said.

"I don't get it." His face scrunched up in a frown.

"Sometimes, words have different meanings. There are lots of words like that, and you'll learn them as you grow big," Ashley explained.

"Okay." He shrugged, apparently bored by the subject already.

"What do you think they are?" David asked.

"Turkey vultures. The wingspan shape as they soar looks like a vee. An eagle has more of a straight line. And the ospreys look more like a W. It's just sometimes hard to get a look from this distance when they're constantly circling and soaring." It was a piece of information she'd picked up in a birding course given by a park ranger, and she'd never forgotten it. The tip came in handy at times like this.

"I'm impressed that you're not jumping to the conclusion they're eagles to prove your point."

Ashley shook her head. "Just because I want something to be true and want to prove it, doesn't mean I make up facts. At some point, it would require proof, of which I wouldn't have. It's a double-edged sword."

"True." David turned to hop off the rock, keeping Cory right with him.

Ashley took her binoculars and scanned the sky, searching the tops of the trees for any sign of a nest or the big white telltale head of a mature eagle, before joining the others. David helped her down and she appreciated the gesture, feeling protected and cherished.

"Your burn line is just over there," she said, pointing to the left. Ashley unfolded the map and then pointed to their current location. "This is where we are. And this is where I need to check. See the problem. If you could just move your line back this way about two miles, it would give me at least the sixteen-square-mile area I originally targeted. And some breathing room for the smoke issues that could arise."

"Two miles?" David took the map from her and studied it. "I had no idea we were talking about that much distance. I can maybe adjust this half a mile max, judging by the contour lines you see here. I'd have to follow this ridgeline. There's nothing like that farther to the left as a natural line to help control the burn."

This wasn't at all what she'd thought would happen. It was bad enough David was going to burn, but now the line she'd hoped she was getting wouldn't be enough. "Are you sure?"

"I'm sure. It's still a compromise." He shrugged. "Let's just keep looking and enjoy the afternoon. Maybe we'll get lucky and find your eagle after all."

"Fine. It's not like I have a choice. And I do appreciate you trying."

"Let me call the chief and see what he says. If he agrees, I'll need to get the guys out here to move the marker lines and dig a new perimeter area. Then we can keep looking for the eagle. I'm in great company, and I couldn't think of a better way to spend my day off." David smiled at her, sending tiny waves of excitement right down to her toes.

"Thank you. Believe it or not, the feeling's mutual," Ashley said, her voice dropping a notch and coming out far huskier than she'd planned. She sounded like a woman in love.

*No. Not again.*

"Trent should be back later today sometime. We need to meet him at O'Malley's at five-thirty to go over the schedule and catch him up on what we've done and what still needs doing." A change in subject was the easiest way to escape David's piercing eyes that noticed far too much.

"Great. Just give me a sec." David stepped off to the side and made a phone call.

Ashley couldn't help but admire the strong set of his shoulders. No matter how hard she'd tried to forget him—moving across the country, starting a new life, and getting married—nothing had changed what was in her heart for the man standing less than twenty feet away.

# Chapter Eleven

♥

SPENDING THE DAY WITH Ashley reminded David of all the fun times they'd shared in the past. Long walks. Hiking. Picnics. Attending games at the school. The school dance. And then there were the times they'd head for the creek to play, or to the pond for a swim. The past replayed like a movie, one of those favorites you could watch over and over.

Their love for the great outdoors had been one of the things that had united them. Obviously, it was still very much a part of their lives, which came as no surprise.

The excitement in her eyes when he'd told her the chief approved the boundary line move was a moment he would have like to capture in a picture. One he would treasure forever, her delight obvious. It was almost the same as each time she shared a picture or pointed out something in the distance for him to check out. *Totally mesmerizing.*

Fun had been in short supply over the years. At first, it had all been about taking care of his mother. And then it had been about moving up the ranks to honor his father's legacy in the fire department. His life had always been about pleasing others, but today, in the here and now, this was for him. And Ashley.

Sharing binoculars brought new meaning to getting a good look. When Ashley was focused on the sky and on the trees beyond, David was focused on her. The soft curve of her face. The way her hair fell loosely around her face in curls, the tendrils licking at her cheeks on a gentle breeze.

And then there was Cory. His boyish charm, excitement, and love for the great outdoors mirrored Ashley's. He also reminded David of a younger version of himself.

Ashley had an incredible eye for knowing what would make a fantastic photograph. When to zoom, how to take advantage of the lighting available to make colors explode on the screen, and even what perspective would capture and hold one's interest.

He'd taken pictures before, but they'd never done justice to the real thing. Ashley's photos were like a breath of fresh air and sunshine, making a person feel like they were right there.

He was enjoying having her in town, even if they weren't on the same side at times. But the ability to wade through issues and come out on top had always been their specialty. Ultimately, they were perfect together.

It was a shame she would be leaving soon, but her dream of joining the National Geographic team was finally within reach. He couldn't think of anyone who deserved a shot at the job more than Ashley.

"Cory, freeze," she whispered. Ashley grabbed his hand, signaling for him to stop, and then pressed a finger to her lips for silence. She pointed off to the right, and David scanned the woods, wondering what she'd seen.

Ashley kneeled, coming shoulder to shoulder with Cory. "Do you see them?" she asked, keeping her voice low. "There's a herd of deer grazing by the pond. Can you see the little ones with spots on them? Those are the babies, and they're called fawns."

"Kojak, sit," David ordered in hushed tones, making sure the dog didn't get wind of them and decide to have a little fun. He put his hand on Ashley's shoulder and squeezed, letting her know he'd spotted the deer.

"They're beautiful, Mommy. Get a picture," Cory said, awe in his voice as he stood perfectly still and watched.

Ashley pressed the viewfinder to her eye, the slight clicking sound made by the shutter letting him know she was getting a lot of photos. They watched and waited, no one moving, enjoying the peaceful serenity of the moment.

A doe's tail shot up and twitched, going into alert mode. The wind must have carried their scent. It wasn't long before the other tails went up in alarm, and the herd started to slink off, their stealthy movements fun to watch. It was as though they thought no one would notice them. Once the deer were out of sight, Ashley lowered her camera. "That was wonderful. I love watching the curiosity a fawn has with each new discovery." She smiled up at him, and David's heart did a summersault.

"Totally." But he was referring more to watching her and enjoying her reaction to what they'd shared.

"I loved the babies, *ummm*, fawns. They were cute. Can we keep going on our adventure walk now?" Cory asked with a renewed zest for what he might find.

"Of course. Take Kojak with you, and don't get too far ahead. You know the rules," Ashley said, making sure they were both on the same page. The kid didn't have to be told twice, and he was off and running.

"You're a great mom, but then I always knew you would be. Cory's a sweet kid and completely like you," David said, not for the first time wondering how things could have been different between them. If only his father hadn't died. Or his mother hadn't shown David the downside of being a firefighter's wife.

"What do you mean?" she asked, looking up at him, a question in her eyes.

"His love for the outdoors. His respect for it. I know he gets that from you." David smiled. "You never could get enough of being outside."

Ashley stopped walking and faced him. "I remember someone else who was the same way. Our careers are different, but both jobs keep us outdoors. We're the same, and yet different. Of course, I get that sometimes your job requires you to do things I could never do."

"Do you? Get it, I mean. I know it's hard sometimes for people to understand how burning an area can help, but there really is a science to it, and it's for the greater good." It was a topic David gave lectures at colleges and to the public, trying to make people understand the reasons for controlled burns. Many people couldn't see past the fact they were burning the woods and displacing animals, bugs, and killing plants and trees. If only things were black and white, but they weren't. Gray definitely came into the picture.

"I get it. The only reason I don't like it is because it's getting in my way." She laughed. Her honesty was refreshing, and so was her support.

An owl hooted nearby. "Did you hear that?" David grinned. "That was a great-horned owl. See, you're not the only one who can identify the sights and sounds out here." David was pleased he'd recognized the bird call. But then he should. He'd heard the sound thousands of times at the visitor center in the park when children pushed the display buttons to listen to all the owl sounds as they tried to identify them.

"Very good. I'm impressed." Ashley nodded, grabbing her binoculars. "Hold up, Cory," she called out.

"Glad to know that's possible." David grinned, her admiration giving him one of those feel-good moments. Standing side by side, he watched her as she searched the treetops for the owl. Watching her bird watch was fast becoming one of his favorite things to do. It gave him the freedom to soak in her beauty without making her uncomfortable. He'd missed her, more than he cared to admit. And for the umpteenth time, he found himself wishing things could be different between them.

She turned to look back at him, a smile on her face. The same smile she'd used as a young woman to wrap him around her little finger. He'd been unable to deny her anything. It was the same smile she'd used just before the first time he ever kissed her. And it was the same smile that made him want to kiss her again.

The sounds of the forest grew silent as he gazed into her eyes. The intensity of the moment reverberated in his head. *Kiss her. Kiss her.*

Ashley wasn't backing away. Did she want him to kiss her? Was it possible she still cared about him even after everything he'd done to drive her away? David leaned forward, making his intentions known, and giving her the chance to end the moment.

She didn't move. If anything, she leaned in closer.

David lost the will to fight what he wanted to do most. Without taking his eyes off her face so he could savor the moment, he lowered his head slowly, anticipation causing his heart to race in triple time.

"Mommy, Mommy! Come quick. Hurry," Cory called out, his voice filled with panic.

They both turned to see what was wrong, but not before David saw the flash of fear in Ashley's eyes. She took off running toward Cory, David, right behind her.

"What's wrong, honey? Did you get stung? Did something bite you? What's wrong?" Ashley asked, her words coming out in a rush as she looked her son over, checking his arms and legs before the kid had a chance to speak.

"No, Mommy. Look. This butterfly can't fly. It's got goopy stuff all over his wings." Cory pointed to the flowering bush he stood next to.

Ashley took a deep breath and let it out. "Oh, thank goodness. Is that all, you're sure? You had me worried." She stood and nodded, her gaze landing on the butterfly and then going back to her son as if to confirm he was okay.

"But, Mommy, this is bad. If the butterfly can't fly, it'll die." His eyes filled up with tears.

Ashley pulled it together and smiled. It was one of those soft and gentle motherly smiles. "You're right, honey. And what a big boy you are to notice the butterfly and recognize he needs help."

"You mean a superhero, right? See, I've got a cape," Cory said, smiling as he held up his cape for inspection.

David grinned; pleased Cory loved his gift.

"You're right. You are a superhero. Maybe we could take the goop off his wings and see if it will help. There's no guarantee, but we sure can try, can't we? We always do our part to help Mother Nature, right?"

"Yup. Gotta try." Cory's smile was firmly back in place.

Ashley was covering all the bases, and David's admiration for her parenting skills rose another notch. His own mother had always been more reliant on his father for everything. She'd never been a take-charge person, which in hindsight was probably why she'd never moved on after his father's death. Ashley wasn't anything like his mother. Instead, she was strong and independent. David couldn't help but wonder if leaving her had been a mistake. Had he destroyed their future out of a fear that all women would be like his mother? It bore considering later, but not now. They had a butterfly to save. "Here," David said, handing her a pair of tweezers from the mini first-aid kit he carried on his belt loop.

"Wow. Look at you, Mr. Boy Scout. This is exactly what we need. Thanks." Ashley's sweet smile reminded him of the almost-kiss they'd missed. Next chance he got, he intended to revisit the option. Hopefully, it would be soon.

Ashley spent the next several minutes pulling spiderweb strings from the butterfly's wings. Piece by piece, she delicately pulled each strand. When the last piece of the web came off, the butterfly turned to face them, still clinging to the flower. It took off and hovered a few seconds, flitting around their heads as if to say thank you.

"We did it, Mommy. Did you see that, Mr. David?" Cory looked up at him, his big blue eyes wide with wonder.

"I did see it. It reminds me of a time when your mommy was a little girl. She had found a lizard without a tail and was determined to save it, thinking it was defenseless. After decorating a cardboard box and turning it into a beautiful nest, she put the lizard in his new home. The next morning, your mom was upset to discover the lizard gone." David grinned at Ashley, the retelling of the memory one that always amused him. There were lots of stories that fell into that category.

"What happened to the lizard?" Cory asked, looking back and forth between him and his mother.

"He crawled out. Lizards lose their tail whenever there's danger. It's a defense mechanism, but it doesn't make them defenseless. They still have four legs and can move pretty quick. And as to their tails, they regrow, usually within a few days. I'm sure Mr. Lizard enjoyed his posh hotel for the night, but he was probably more than ready to return to his family the next day." David winked at Ashley.

"It's not like anybody told me," Ashley said in defense, a slight blush tinging her cheeks.

"You're right, we didn't. We were having too much fun watching you play mother to a lizard," David teased. He and Trent had done that a lot. It was only about the time Ashley turned sixteen when he'd realized his feelings were anything but sisterly, and that he'd fallen in love with her.

*Something that had never changed.*

# Chapter Twelve

♥

ASHLEY COULDN'T BELIEVE DAVID had almost kissed her. *Saved by a bug.* The question was, did she want to be saved? The answer needed to be yes, because letting herself care about David would be foolhardy. And it was something she'd sworn to never let happen again. Life was about moving forward. That meant leaving Hallbrook, and with any luck, heading to D.C. for her dream job.

A knock on the door startled her. She wasn't expecting anyone, and she didn't have time for visitors. She and Cory needed to get cleaned up and changed to meet Trent and David in town tonight.

Ashley was thrilled when she discovered her surprise visitor was Trent. She threw herself at him, realizing just how much she'd missed him over the years. Computer chats just weren't the same as a good old-fashion hug. "You're here!"

"I am. I wrapped up some things faster than I thought I could and wanted to surprise you." He grinned, stepping back to get a good look at her. "And from what I hear, it's a good thing I'm back."

Her brother looked good in a suit and tie, not something she'd seen very often growing up. No wonder the judge's daughter was interested. Trent was a handsome, successful guy.

"Hi, Uncle Trent," Cory said, hugging his uncle's leg.

"Hey there, kiddo. You sure look bigger and taller from the last time I saw you on video chat." Trent ruffled Cory's hair, something lots of people couldn't resist because of her son's thick curls.

"Talking on the computer makes everybody look small. You were only this big," Cory said, holding up his hands to indicate the size of the computer screen.

Trent laughed. "Good point."

"Watch this, Uncle Trent. I'm a big boy now, and I can do a handstand." Cory moved to the center of the living room and proceeded to show his new acrobatic abilities. Her son hadn't stopped practicing them since Chloe showed him while he was over at Tricia's, but his little legs and arm strength weren't enough to make the move into anything more than what appeared to be a floundering fish.

"What did you mean when you said it sounded like it was 'a good thing you're back'?" Her curiosity about his comment wouldn't let her dismiss it without an explanation.

"I stopped at the post office to get my mail and got an ear full. Is there something going on between you and David?" Trent drilled her with a look that gave her pause. It was almost as if he wasn't happy about what he'd heard.

Not that the rumor was true, but still, why wouldn't Trent want his best friend and his sister to be together? He hadn't said a thing when they were kids, so why now? "You know the Hallbrook gossip chain. It's normally more gossip than fact."

"Normally, but I know you two had a thing a long time ago." Again, it wasn't his words that worried her, but the way he said them. There was something odd going on.

Ashley shook her head, trying to reassure her overprotective brother. "It was a long time ago. David and I are just friends now."

Trent snorted. "*Just friends* doesn't describe what I've been hearing. It sounds like you two can't decide between being enemies or lovers."

"We are neither. Just because we went up against each other in court doesn't mean we weren't civil about it. He even tried to help me find the eagles today. So don't worry too much about it. I'm sure you heard I lost the injunction hearing, but I appreciate everything you did to try and help me."

"I did hear," Trent said, turning back to watch Cory, and clapping on cue. "How are you handling that? I know you hate to lose, and I know your motive is pure."

"I'm okay. David offered a compromise to move the line. It's not enough, but every little bit helps. Ideally, the burn needs to be put on hold for another week or so. The smoke will drive the eagles away if it gets too close. I feel like there's something else I need to be doing, but I don't think I have a choice other than to give up."

Her brother grinned. "The judge's orders are pretty solid. I'd hate to see my sister end up in the slammer."

Ashley nudged her brother's shoulder with her own. "I wouldn't go that far, and you know it. I have Cory to think about." It was good to see Trent again, the teasing reminding her of the fun they once had.

"Good. I'm not ready to take on the responsibility of playing daddy while you're an inmate." Trent ducked and moved away, avoiding the punch she was about to land against his shoulder. All in fun, of course.

"Well, I hope you are ready to step up for your responsibility toward the festival. We've been picking up your share of the load while you were out having a good time wining and dining clients," Ashley teased.

Cory came racing back to stand next to them, his breathing fast from all the gymnastics. "Did you see my handstand, Uncle Trent?"

Trent smiled. "I did, buddy. I think you can do them better than I can."

David chose that moment to step into the open doorway. "Knock. Knock," he said, tapping on the wood to announce his presence.

"Hey there, we were just talking about you," Trent said, reaching out to shake hands.

David's left eyebrow shot up. "I bet you were. Glad you're back in town. Somehow, it seems like you never left," he said dryly.

"What's that supposed to mean?" Trent frowned.

David shot him a glare. "Only that even out of town, it would appear you can pull some strings."

Trent, in turn, glared at her. "Thanks for not saying anything, sis."

Ashley crossed her heart. "I didn't." It was an old sign they'd used as kids to symbolize they were telling the truth. Kind of like a pinky swear, only stronger.

David shook his head. "It wasn't rocket science to figure it out. Very few people could pull something like that off at the last minute."

"True." Trent shrugged. "No hard feelings?"

"No. We're behind a couple of days, but the burn starts tomorrow. Our concern was getting it done before the upcoming holiday. With this many people coming in from the cities to camp, there's an increased chance for wildfires. On the upside, I got to spend the day with Ashley and Cory out in the woods. A very special day indeed." David winked at her, but luckily, Trent didn't see it, or there might have been more disapproving looks. Not to mention questions she didn't want to answer.

"Is that a fact?" Trent asked, picking up Cory, but his gaze never leaving David.

"That's a fact." The two men squared off, leaving Ashley to wonder yet again what was going on between them.

Time for a change in subject. "We need to set up a couple of booths. David and I hung the flyers and worked on the signs. Even Cory got to help with the artwork. But three people working will make the booths easier to put up. They're big and bulky," Ashley interjected, bringing the conversation back to why they were meeting in the first place.

"Yeah, I heard you and Ashley got quite a bit done. Together." Trent scowled.

David tensed, but he wasn't backing down. "And your point?"

*So much for a change in subject.*

"I just remember a conversation you and I had once upon a time. I didn't realize anything had changed." Trent glanced her way and then back at David, raising Ashley's suspicions.

Enough was enough. "What are you guys talking about?" she asked, straight and to the point.

"Nothing," they both said in unison—more reason for her not to believe them. Trent would have some explaining to do later.

"Then let's get over to the fairgrounds and get started. We can grab some pizza after we knock out the first booth. The sooner we get started, the sooner we get done." And the sooner she could drag the information out of Trent.

"Sounds like a plan," David said. "Give me ten minutes to let Kojak out for a quick run."

"I want to go with Mr. David to see Kojak. Please, Mommy, can I?" Cory begged.

"That's fine. But make sure you mind him."

Trent set Cory down, and her son grabbed David's hand as they headed out the door. He was becoming attached to David, which wasn't necessarily good. And yet somehow, Ashley couldn't think of it as bad either.

She turned away, but not before glancing at Trent. He was watching her and the now empty doorway with a scowl on his face. Ashley was of a mind to stay home and let the two of them duke it out—whatever *it* was.

Ashley worked up a sweat as the three of them hammered the corner poles into the ground. Finally, they added the walls and ceiling and zipped them all into place. The process was archaic compared to the newfangled easy-up tents sold everywhere. Clearly, Hallbrook didn't have the funds to update the equipment.

Too bad she hadn't known that before she agreed to put them up. The sandbags were the last things to be attached. *One down, two to go.*

*And time for pizza.* "I've got to get Cory something to eat. Do you all want to take a break and head to O'Malley's, or do you want to keep working, and I can bring something back?" Ashley was hoping they pick the second option and keep working. That way, they'd get the next one down and she'd be off the hook for helping. Trent and David looked at each other and shrugged as if they didn't care one way or the other.

"We'll keep going. Consider it my penance for missing the earlier stuff," Trent volunteered.

Exactly what she wanted to hear. "I'll go pick up a pizza and bring it back."

"Sounds good," David said, reaching for his wallet.

"I've got this." Things might be tight, but she didn't want to come across as desperate. Not in front of Trent or David, the two men she cared the most about in her life. "Come on, Cory. Let's go get dinner."

It was a short walk to O'Malley's. Ashley led Cory inside, keeping hold of his hand as she made her way to an empty table by the bar. It would be a good place to sit and wait for the pizza to cook.

Melissa, one of the servers, came to take her order.

"I'll take a large pepperoni pizza and a large onion and mushroom pizza, please. Oh, and it's to go," Ashley added.

"Anything to drink with that?" the woman asked.

"Yes, please. Four ice teas. Thanks." It had been a long day and a glass of wine would be nice, but with Cory here, she wouldn't give in to the act of self-indulgence.

"That'll take about twenty minutes. Okay?" Melissa asked.

Ashley nodded. "Absolutely." She sat back to look around the place, curious who was here and who she'd recognize.

Cory went into talk mode, asking her questions about everything he saw. She didn't mind answering because she liked the inquisitive side of her son—something else Joe hadn't appreciated at all.

"Hi, Ashley. I didn't expect to see you here tonight, not with the burn starting tomorrow." Tricia came and stood next to her.

"Don't remind me," she said, shaking her head. "What are you doing here? I thought you were overrun by family at home?"

Tricia let out a deep breath. "I refused to cook and do dishes for this crowd one more night without a break, so we all came out to eat. They're all over there." Her friend pointed to a large table in the corner. "I saw you come in and wanted to come say hi."

"I don't blame you." Ashley laughed.

"Am I coming to play tomorrow, Miss Tricia?" Cory asked. "I missed Chloe and Bryan today."

"That's up to your mother, but you're always welcome." Tricia grinned at Cory.

"Can I, Mommy?" he asked, not letting the matter drop.

"We shall see. Let's get through tonight first." She leaned over to kiss the top of his head.

"I'm sorry about the injunction. I know you had your heart set on winning and having more time to find the eagle," Tricia said.

"Me, too. But there's nothing else I can do. Unless... A crazy idea popped into her head. Maybe it was time to take charge of her own life and stop letting people dictate the outcome for her.

"Unless what?" Tricia asked, a worried frown appearing suddenly.

"What if we put together a protest?" Crazy was an understatement, but it didn't stop her from getting excited about the possibility.

Tricia's eyes danced with merriment. "You can be like those people on TV and lay yourself down at the bottom of the fire truck, you know, so they can't move forward."

Ashley laughed, sobering only as she pictured David's face if she did something else to disrupt his plans. "That might be a bit extreme."

"I know. But you could form a picket line. Judging by some of the things I've heard from the people in town, you wouldn't have a hard time putting together one. Lots of folks here are keen on you finding the eagle." Tricia nodded.

"You're kidding?" Ashley had no idea the town was even talking about what she was doing, much less rooting for her. She'd only told a few of them what she was up to.

"Nope. It would be a huge honor and a claim to fame for our little town." Tricia stood as if to leave.

"You don't say." Ashley's brain was spinning a mile a minute as the idea of a picket line percolated. "A peaceful protest isn't against the law, and it might be just what we need."

A worried look crossed her friend's face. "I was half teasing."

"Maybe. But think about it, picket lines normally attract the media. And if we get the attention of the media, public opinion might sway the fire department." Ashley came alive, her weariness vanishing in a split second.

Tricia nodded. "It might work and be worth a shot. Is there anything I can do to help?"

"Spread the word. The fire department is supposed to be at the North Summit entrance at six a.m. I saw some of the equipment parked and ready to go. If we show up at five-thirty, we can form a line and stop them." Ashley wished both her and David could win this battle, but unfortunately, it didn't work that way. David would be furious. She totally understood his position and understood that public safety was important. But this was important too, for her and the bald eagle.

"Who's the editor for the *Hallbrook Daily Times*?"

"That would be Mabel Avery. She's over there eating dinner with her husband." Tricia pointed to a couple across the room.

"You know everybody here better than I do. If you spread the word, I will talk to Mabel." The renewed hope of stalling the burn filled her with joy. "I prefer to surprise David and Trent with our plans, so let's not say anything yet." Ashley winked and nodded to

Cory. She'd have to do her best to keep them apart, or her son would let the fire out of the dragon, so to speak.

Trent and David would find out her plans soon enough come morning.

# Chapter Thirteen

♥

D AVID CHECKED OVER HIS notes and the details for the burn one last time as he finished his coffee. There was no room for mistakes. They were on a tight schedule to get as much done as possible in a short amount of time because of all the delays.

He grabbed his jacket off the coat hook and tossed it in the truck. The crisp morning air in the mountains could be chilly even though it was summer. Kojak followed him out the door, stopping briefly at one of the bushes before hopping in the truck. The dog took up his usual post in the front passenger seat, determined to look out the window. David reached over to pat him on the head before backing out of the driveway.

As he drove off, he couldn't shake the feeling he'd forgotten something. Or something was out of place. He retraced his steps from this morning in his head, trying to jog his memory.

*Ashley's car.* It hadn't been there this morning when he left. She'd probably stayed at Trent's last night, and there was nothing to worry about. Except when it concerned Ashley, he always worried.

Obviously, that hadn't changed.

Twenty minutes later, he pulled into the North Summit entrance, where the staging area for the burn had been set up. He was surprised to see several cars already parked along the road, some of the guys beating him here. Except, he didn't recognize the cars as those of his crew.

A sixth sense something was about to go wrong took hold and wouldn't let go, the feeling starting in the pit of his stomach and traveling up to his throat. He pulled in next to one of the fire trucks and got out, letting Kojak follow.

His gaze landed on Ashley's car, and his sixth sense moved into factual information territory. There was no way Ashley was here bright and early this morning to cheer him on—which could only mean one thing. *Trouble.*

David glanced around, the hairs on the back of his neck standing on end. He spotted a group of people, none of whom were dressed in firefighter gear. The group stood in a line blocking his fire trucks, each person carrying a sign. The messages ranged from "stop the burn" to "eagles matter" to "save the eagle."

*Unbelievable. A picket line.*

Of all the crazy notions she could have come up with, this one irritated him the most. Picket lines always seemed to bring in the media. And when that happened, nobody won.

David needed to speak with her and try to stop this nonsense before it got out of hand. He spotted her in a group with some of the others in line and made his way to her side.

"Ashley, can we talk? Privately," David urged, hoping she'd agree to a peaceful end to this.

"I'm staying right here. Anything you have to say, my friends can hear too." Ashley stood taller, but he hadn't missed the almost imperceptible hesitation before she spoke.

"You can't do this, and you know it. The judge denied the injunction." David started counting, trying to diffuse his anger. It wouldn't help the situation, and he was trying to keep the communication lines open.

"We can, and we will. It's called freedom of speech, and it's a peaceful protest."

"The burn is scheduled to begin in thirty minutes, and we can't have people getting in the way and possibly getting hurt. You all need to move out of the staging area. This area is closed to the public."

"I'm just asking for another week or so," she said, defiance and hope all rolled into the one sentence.

"And I've explained to you that's time we don't have. This holiday week is one of the most dangerous weeks when it comes to forest fires. Casually tossed cigarette butts, fires not properly put out, hikers starting small fires that get out of control. There are a dozen things that can go wrong when people start having fun, or drinking, and aren't as careful as they should be."

"I get it. I really do, and I'm sorry we disagree over this. If people outside of Hallbrook get word about the possible eagle here, it might just bring people in by the droves and we would stand a better chance of someone spotting it. If you burn, the eagles will leave. And if you burn, nobody will want to hike a blackened and charred area. You'll be a hero if we find the eagle."

David shook his head. "I'm not looking to be a hero. I'm looking to protect the community and the White Mountain National Forest. Some hero I'll be if we have a wildfire that burns out of control because I didn't do my job."

"We both need to do what we believe is right." Ashley raised her sign higher in defiance as if to prove her point.

"Are you going to move out of the staging area or not?" David glared.

"Probably not." Ashley looked away, unable to meet his gaze. She wasn't going to give in without resistance.

His crew started to arrive, and soon, the place would be teeming with firefighters ready to get to work.

"What's going on, Chief Beckett?" Captain James asked, having volunteered to help and coordinate activities in the staging area.

"Ashley Stanton organized a picket line." He frowned at her, making sure she knew he was giving her full credit for this nonsense.

"Trouble we don't need. Want me to call it in?" Captain James asked.

David wasn't quite ready to go that far. He needed to give Ashley and the others another chance to make the right choice. "I'll call it in. I'm going to try talking to them some more. Get everything ready to go. The burn will go on as scheduled."

"Yes, sir." Captain James and the others wandered off and headed for their trucks. He watched as the men began to suit up and start to lay out the hoses.

David turned back to Ashley. "Time's up for you and your friends. You need to leave the designated areas that are officially closed to visitors, or I'll have no choice but to call the sheriff's department and have you all removed and charged with trespassing."

Ashley's mouth dropped open in surprise. "You wouldn't dare." She glared back at him, her steely gaze not quite as defiant as moments ago.

"Try me." David had lost all patience. He appreciated what Ashley was trying to do, but she'd lost, and she wasn't doing it very graciously. There was no way he would put the department's agenda on hold until she was satisfied there was no eagle. There had to be some balance, and David hadn't made it to battalion chief by kowtowing to pressure. Ashley had had her chance and failed.

David turned and headed back for his truck. He suited up in his fire gear, checking and double-checking all his equipment. Not much of a behind-the-lines type of guy, today he'd be out there with the crew, unwilling to ask them to do anything he wasn't willing to do himself. He didn't like moving the line at the last minute, and Ashley's attitude made him wish he hadn't done it. He'd reviewed the maps last night, trying to memorize every detail of the change, and he knew the challenges they faced today.

He glanced at his watch and then at Ashley and the group of picketers. It was past time for them to be gone. David pulled out his phone and dialed the sheriff's office. He'd deal with the fallout with

Ashley and Trent and the rest of the town later. Right now, he had a job to do.

Empowered by the community, Ashley refused to budge. It didn't mean she wasn't nervous, but she didn't go all weak and become a pushover. The picket line was about making a point, not making David mad. But she'd seen the look in his eyes and knew he was disappointed, and she knew he was more than justified. She *had* used the injunction to get her way, and it had failed. Now, she was resorting to other means to stop the burn. But she was also losing valuable time in her search.

Maybe her overzealous search to find the eagle had been for all the wrong reasons. Maybe it was about more than just finding the eagle. And more than a welcome addition to her portfolio. Maybe it was about discovering herself in the process and wanting to get something right for once in her life.

Her father had been controlling, acting as though nothing she did was good enough for him. After he died, Trent had taken his place. Even David had been the one to make the decision to end things between them. He'd changed the direction of her life without so much as a discussion. And then there was Joe. Her husband had wooed her and told her everything she needed to hear, and when he'd proposed, she said yes. From the minute she'd said I do, Joe had controlled all the decisions. Where they went, who they saw. Everything.

It was just a repeating pattern, and Ashley was tired of it. She wanted to take a stand. Not to be weak. Just this once, she didn't want life to happen to her, she wanted to take charge and make it happen.

"Don't worry about him," one of the women standing next to her said. "He'll get over it. I see the way he looks at you, and this—" the woman waved her hand toward the group, "—won't change how he feels. At least he'll know better than to take you for granted," the woman said, a wide grin on her face. "It's not like we didn't all know we couldn't win. This is only about taking a stand. Thank you for letting us do this with you, Ashley. We know there are people on both sides of the line, but it makes us feel better to know we tried. Is there any harm in that?"

"No, none." The woman was right about the reasons they were doing this, but she was all wrong about her and David. They were friends. That was all they ever could be, especially with her leaving.

*But what about the almost kiss?*

Clearly, they still had feelings for one another. Or maybe it was a simple matter of attraction. Yes, that's precisely what it was. Attraction.

"So, when do you think we should leave?" another woman asked just as the fire truck engines began roaring to life.

"Now would be a good time," the first woman said. "The last thing I need is to get arrested."

The three of them turned and watched as the Channel 9 News van pulled into the parking lot. A man with an oversized camera jumped out and began filming. A second man exited the vehicle and headed in their direction. He shoved a microphone toward them. "Channel 9 News, Brent Maddox reporting. Can you tell me who's directing this picket?"

"I am," Ashley said nervously, glancing around to find David. Her hopes the news media would show up had materialized, which meant the picket line would make the news. Now, she wasn't so sure about this. But one thing was for sure, she'd come too far to back down.

"Would you mind answering a few questions?" the young reporter asked.

"Go ahead. But just one minute." She looked over at the woman standing next to her, "I guess this answers your question. We'll stick around for a little while longer and see what happens."

"This is fun," the woman said, chuckling. "Reminds me of the time the high-school girls staged a sit-in at the cafeteria when the school administration wanted to remove the bathroom doors in the girl's bathroom. We won. Maybe we'll get lucky and win today, too. The news media is certainly an interesting twist."

The reporter stuck a microphone in her face. "Who are you, and what are you trying to accomplish here today?"

"I'm Ashley Stanton, and I'm investigating a bald eagle sighting reported to the Audubon Society. The area we believe the eagle might be in coincides with the fire department's controlled burn. The burn could displace the eagle and his mate if he has one. A fire could also destroy any nest they have, and possibly cause harm to any immatures born in the last seven or eight weeks. I simply need more time to complete my search before they do the controlled burn.

"This would be an amazing discovery for Hallbrook if we have a nesting pair of eagles who have established a home here." Ashley clutched her sign to hide her nerves. She'd always been the one behind the camera and she wasn't nearly as confident being the one filmed. She tried to maintain a sense of calm, wanting to answer the man's questions to the best of her abilities.

"Bald eagles are federally protected. What seems to be the problem?" the reporter asked.

"They are. The problem rests in the fact that I haven't come across any evidence yet, other than the reported sighting, of course. And without evidence, there is nothing to protect." And there was the entire problem wrapped up neatly in a pinecone.

"Have you tried asking for more time?" It was a foolish question, but she understood he was just covering the bases.

"I have. I tried to get an injunction, but the judge ruled against me. The picket line is to let the fire department and those in charge know that it's more than just me who believes in the importance of using every means possible to find the eagle. Our community is urging them to hold up for a week or so. That's all." Sirens in the distance sent chills down her spine. David had made good on his threat.

"Well, by the sounds of things, you haven't managed to change their minds. It looks like they're ready to roll and have called in reinforcements. What will you do when they arrive?"

The cameraman panned the group of picketers, then the group of firefighters standing off to the side waiting for orders, and then turned back to her as they waited for her answer.

"This is a peaceful protest to make sure the fire department knows the community is against their decision. Mission accomplished. Chief Beckett told us he would call the sheriff, and apparently, he's a man of his word." She grinned. "And since none of us are looking to get arrested, that would be our cue to leave."

"Sounds like a good idea." The reporter smiled back at her and nodded. He moved off, the cameraman close on his heels, as he went to talk to some of the others as the p picket group disbanded. Two police cars pulled into the parking area, lights flashing and sirens wailing. Four uniformed officers got out of the vehicles and surveyed the scene.

Captain Taylor made his way to her side. Ashley was acutely aware of the gun and handcuffs he wore even though she knew they were a standard part of a police-officers uniform. "You know you shouldn't be here, right?"

"That's debatable." Ashley shrugged.

"Can I take it by what I see that you're all leaving peacefully?" Captain Taylor asked.

"Yes. We're satisfied that by this evening, the entire state will know that some of us would have liked to have seen a different outcome today."

Captain Taylor nodded. "I'm glad to hear you've decided to cooperate. I'd hate to have to haul you down to the station."

"I'd hate for you to have to do that, too." Ashley winked and walked off to her car. She took one last glance at David, surprised to discover him watching her. Even more surprised when he nodded in her direction. Proud she'd stood up for herself or pleased she was leaving?

*Most likely, the latter.*

Ashley sat in her car for a few moments, watching as some of the firefighters headed into the woods, David amongst them. A few others stayed back, directing everyone out of the area. She said a prayer for David and the other firefighter's safety, and hoping the burn went well. She may have been a thorn in David's side, but her heart was securely in the right place.

David was her friend. Once upon a time, more than a friend. Who was she kidding? Recently, her thoughts turned to mush as she found herself attracted to him once again. The trouble was—nothing had changed for David. The man was still a loner and against relationships.

The sooner she left Hallbrook the better because Ashley wasn't sure she'd survive a second time around broken heart when it came to David.

# Chapter Fourteen

♥

ASHLEY HEADED BACK TOWARD town. Spending the rest of the day with Cory was precisely what she needed to take her mind off the burn—and the eagle.

Several deep breaths later, she felt the tension ebbing from her body. Usually, she was rushing from point A to point B, so when she spotted a sign for a scenic vista turnout, she opted to take advantage of the free moment.

She slid out of the car and walked up to the stone wall. Letting her gaze scan the wide expanse, she drank in the beauty. The mountain tops rose majestically not far from here, and the valley dipped below where she spotted several farms, houses, and barns. Christmas Tree Lane was the only access to the area off the main road that led to Hallbrook if she remembered correctly.

In the distance, she spotted an oversized bird kettling through the skies, enjoying the light breeze. More than likely, just another vulture. She'd seen her share of those recently. In her haste to leave this morning, she'd left her binoculars and camera on the kitchen table, assuming she wouldn't need them at the picket site.

Always a mistake, one she vowed to never repeat. You never knew when they'd come in handy. Like now.

The vulture soared closer and closer. The bird's markings were not yet definable, but the wingspan line was more distinct. And it wasn't a V, of that she was sure. The question was, was the shape a straight line or the slight W of an osprey.

Her heart started to race as she wondered if this was the eagle. Of all the foolish times to leave her equipment at home, this one took first place. Ashley willed the bird to fly closer, hoping to get a good view, one that might define the markings and identity of her feathered friend.

Closer and closer he came, circling the skies. Specks of white broke the solid black image, proof it wasn't a vulture. It was the head of the bird that was white. This was the eagle she'd been searching for. She pulled out her phone and tried to magnify the view, hoping to capture a picture as evidence it wasn't an osprey. She tried to zoom in and out repeatedly, but the focus didn't catch. The pictures were grainy, and the bird remained unrecognizable. But Ashley was sure in her heart it was the eagle.

It was a sign she needed to keep looking. The area was southeast of where David and his crew were doing the burn and it's not like she'd be interfering. A plan came to mind, one that involved Trent for a couple of reasons. One, she didn't want to leave this spot, thinking it better to keep an eye on the bird. And two, she needed him to grab her equipment, meet up with her, and join her on the search. Trent would provide protection from David's wrath if he discovered she'd been out in the woods after he'd told her to leave.

Her brother answered on the first ring. "Hey, there. It's Ashley," she said, skipping preliminaries.

"Morning to you, too," Trent teased.

"I don't have time for pleasantries. I'm on a mission, and I need your help." She was banking on her brother's protective streak to keep him from saying no.

"Why do I have a feeling this isn't going to be good?"

"I want you to go with me to search for the eagle today." Ashley debated just how much to tell him. The last thing she needed was for him to dig in and not only say no, but heck no. Because then he'd find a way to stop her as well.

"And why do you suddenly need a chaperone? You've been out searching a few times on your own already." Trent's voice had grown tense. Her brother was all too familiar with her tactics from when they were growing up.

"Because I'm trying to be smart. The fire department is doing the controlled burn today. And although they're far enough away from where I will be, I just thought the buddy system would be a good precaution. Not to mention, I need you to pick up my camera and binoculars."

"I don't like the sound of this. That area will be off-limits if it's anywhere nearby, and you know it."

Trent was digging in his feet, but Ashley still had an ace in the hole. Trent's overprotective side.

"I'm at the scenic overlook just before you enter the park, and I'm watching a bird in the distance that from what I can tell is a bald eagle. I need to get over to the South Summit area and look around ASAP. I'm going. The only question is whether you're coming with me."

"Do I have a choice?" His voice had changed to one of resignation, and Ashley knew she'd won even before he answered.

"Not if you don't want me to go alone."

"David's going to kill me for helping you do this, but since you leave me no choice, I guess I'll see you in about twenty minutes."

"David's too busy to be worried about what we're doing. Besides, they are up at the North Summit area." It was the truth, although it wouldn't stay that way. She knew the one of the perimeters was part way between the North and South Summit parking lots. Something she had no intention of pointing out. "Maybe the reason I spotted the eagle this morning versus all the other times I've been out here is because of the burn. The smoke could be making him nervous. And if that's true, the eagle will leave."

"I hope you know what you're doing or the both of us could end up in jail."

"It'll be fine. Oh, I just thought of something. I need to meet you at the apartment. You don't have a key." This would set her back almost forty-five minutes—time she didn't have to spare.

"Lucky for you, I have a key. I took care of something for David's mother once and never remembered to give back the spare."

"That's wonderful. See, it's another sign," Ashley said, anxious to start searching.

"You and your signs. You've gone crazy trying to find this eagle. I don't know what's going on in your head, but I'm not sure I like it. You used to be more levelheaded and rational."

"There's nothing irrational about trying to save an eagle," Ashley said, defending her actions.

"Why do I sense there's more to it than this?" Trent's question caught her off guard since it was the very same question she'd asked herself earlier.

"There's not. See you soon." She hung up the phone, not wanting to delve into the matter too far. Not now, anyway. Maybe later, when she was alone.

Twenty-five minutes later, Trent pulled into the scenic turnout. The bird had long since disappeared, but that didn't change her determination to search. He got out of his car and joined her, bringing her camera and binoculars.

"Are you sure I can't talk you out of this?" he asked, shooting her one of his big-brother frowns.

"No. And now that you're here, I should tell you something else." They got in her car, and Ashley put the car in reverse, easing out of the parking space. "Better from me than on the news." She winced, knowing his reaction wouldn't be a good one. She turned in the direction of the park, intent on seeing this through.

"Oh, no, what did you do?" Trent asked, his voice sterner than she'd heard in a long time.

"A few locals joined me this morning in a protest at the burn site. It started peacefully and ended peacefully, so don't go getting all cranked up and crazy on me. It's just when the news media showed up, we stayed a little longer to tell our side of the story."

"Good grief, Ashley. You've gone too far, this time." Trent shook his head, frustration evident in every line of his face.

She turned back to watch the road, hating that her brother was upset with her, but knowing it had been the right thing to do. They'd only wanted to express their opinions—and they hadn't gotten in the way. Where was the harm in that?

"It wasn't so bad, and it ended well after the sheriff showed up. So, you have nothing to worry about."

"The sheriff?" Trent asked, his voice tight with tension. "You do realize I'm dating the judge's daughter? And that you had me call in a favor for that injunction. This is not going to look good. You need to stop involving me in your plans. This is the last time; do you hear me? I'm done with this craziness. You need to let it go."

Ashley knew she'd pushed him too far, and he was probably right. "Or maybe, you just need to stop worrying so much."

"Maybe I could if you'd figure out how to stay out of trouble. Between fending off boyfriends, making sure you finished high school, having you run off to California and marry and divorce some jerk, worry is my middle name. And now, you're back in Hallbrook with no job, and from what I can tell, limited resources. At what point do you think I can stop worrying?"

Put like that, it sounded terrible. But not everyone's life was quiet and uneventful like his. Or how his might have been until she'd come back to town. "Nobody asked you to worry." Ashley stiffened, taking offense at the idea his protective streak was something he resented.

"After dad died, I did." Trent nodded. "Mom told me once I would have to be the man of the house. It stuck, and I did everything I could to make her happy. I hated that she was hurt and alone." His voice had grown raw with emotion, and Ashley didn't have to look at him to see the pain.

"I'm sorry. That's a heavy load, especially when you were only fourteen. What did you mean about driving off my boyfriends? It's not like I dated much." Ashley pulled into the South Summit entrance and parked, ignoring the roadblock and simply driving around it. What the fire department didn't know wouldn't hurt anyone.

"Forget I said that," Trent said, snapping out of the dark place he'd gone.

"No, what did you mean? I didn't know you'd interfered in my love life. I would've had a few things to say about that if I'd known. You had no right." Ashley frowned. Trent didn't say a word about the roadblock, leading her to believe wherever he'd gone mentally had blocked out everything else around him temporarily.

"Maybe not, but it was my job as your big brother and the father figure in the house," Trent insisted, getting out of the car and following her to the trailhead.

"Exactly how many boyfriends did you run off? I don't remember too many boys even showing interest." Ashley stopped walking, determined to know the truth. It was her life, and clearly, he'd interfered.

"Just one, as it turns out." Trent shrugged and kept walking, avoiding her gaze.

"And who was he? Randy Thompson? I thought he was going to ask me to the prom senior year, but that never happened. Did you get to him first?" she persisted, her anger simmering just below a boil. It shouldn't matter, as it was ages ago, but it did. After David's betrayal, Randy's sudden lack of interest had hurt more than she cared to admit.

Trent stopped, turning back to look at her. He let out a deep breath. "You don't want to know. It was a long time ago, and it doesn't matter now. You should just forget I even let it slip."

"Who, Trent?" She grabbed his arm, determined not to let him walk away this time.

He glanced down to where she held him and then looked back at her. "David."

That one word had the power to shock her to the very core of her being. It was the last name she'd expected to hear. "I don't understand. He was your best friend. Why would you run him off?" It was impossible. Her brother's confession meant David ditching her hadn't been his decision.

"When I found out the two of you were more than friends, it drove me crazy. I was the typical big brother who didn't want anyone dating his little sister, especially not his best friend.  I knew exactly how Dad must have felt watching you grow up and worrying about you dating. I saw how controlling he was with you, but I understood. Besides, David has relationship issues. I've known him a long time, and he isn't the committing type.  Not then, and not now. I wasn't going to let him stick around to break your heart. And he's proven me right. After all these years, he still hasn't settled down with anyone." Trent raised his chin just a notch, but enough to let her know he felt justified, and that sent her over the top.

"How dare you! He broke my heart, and now I find out it was all your fault. How could you do this to me?" Ashley's chest clenched, her heart agonizing as old wounds resurfaced.

Some of Trent's other comments filtered through her brain. Trent was responsible for David dumping her, that was clear. But David was the one who'd allowed her brother to push him around and dictate their relationship, not bothering to fight for her. He'd seen it as an opportunity to run. She was angry with her brother, but after several deep breaths, she tried to rein it in. It wasn't important anymore. And knowing the truth made it easier to put an end to any fanciful notions she had about David every time he walked into the room.

"I did it for your own good. Like I said, water under the bridge. Let it go. And nothing's changed. I don't want to see you get your heart broken again. Stay away from him, Ashley."

"You have nothing to fear on that score. Come on, we need to get a move on." She pulled out the map and checked her coordinates along the way, heading in the same direction she'd seen bird last fly off.

They spent the next hour searching deeper into the gridded area she'd highlighted. Ashley stopped to rub her neck, lifting her hair. The cool breeze felt good against the sweat on her neck. The smell of smoke was faint in the air, reminding her that not far from here, David and the fire department were hard at work. Now more than ever, she was grateful he'd agreed to move the perimeter lines.

She and Trent continued to search, and it was like old times when the two of them used to pal around together. Pushing aside their differences, she started to relax, enjoying her time with Trent. Her brother had a big heart, something she needed to remember. Anything he'd done, he'd done out of love, even if he'd been mistaken.

"Look over there." Trent pointed up at the sky behind them, and the air of fun dissipated and was replaced by concern. "It looks like some of the smoke is billowing in this direction. I hadn't noticed that before."

"Neither did I. The wind is blowing in a southerly direction, toward us. Earlier, it was blowing in the opposite direction." Wisps of gray smoke flitted through the trees and across the skyline.

"With the fire department burning upwind of us, the smoke could get thicker. Maybe we should head back now to play it safe." Trent was the voice of reason, and Ashley was almost inclined to agree.

*Almost.*

The change in wind direction would not be good news for the fire department. David had repeatedly told her that details and timing were critical in a controlled burn. She couldn't imagine they'd planned for shifting winds, not to mention the wind speed seemed to have picked up. "Let's keep looking a bit longer. There's a ridge just a little way from here. We'll turn around there and head back."

"First sensible thing I've heard you say all day," Trent said, his boyish grin took the sting out of the words.

# Chapter Fifteen

♥

D AVID WATCHED AS HIS guys set the mini fires, each person knowing exactly what to do. They needed to work together as a team. The burn was systematically managed, and as they moved forward, they checked and rechecked to make sure everything stayed under control.

"Watch that backline, Bart," David called out. One of the fires wasn't dying down as quickly as expected. It was best to keep everything low and tight, using the gentle wind to move the blaze northward in the direction planned.

"Ten-four, Chief Beckett," Bart answered through the headset they all wore for communication.

A bird flew overhead. David glanced up as much for himself as for Ashley. If he spotted an eagle, he'd call the burn off in a heartbeat. The bird flew closer, and David recognized it as a vulture.

He returned his focus to the fire as the heat grew more intense. David opened his jacket a little to let more air in and then used the bandana around his neck to wipe the sweat off his brow.

"How's it look from your side, Chief Beckett?" Captain James asked over the headset.

"Looking good. It seems the breeze has picked up, but it's moving the fire in the right direction, and everything's still manageable. Wouldn't hurt to check with NOAA for an updated weather report." David glanced up at the treetops, reconfirming his assessment.

"Will do," Captain James answered.

David stayed ahead of the crew, checking the twenty-foot wide path cleared at the perimeter to control sparks from jumping the original line, setting off unintended burns that could quickly get out of control. The newest section of freshly cleared ground wasn't as deep as he would have liked it since the change was only implemented yesterday, but at least there was no brush, and there should be adequate protection.

The chatter in the headset continued as the crew worked together to control the burn.

"Chief Beckett," Captain James broke in over the airway. "I just got the update from NOAA, and it's not good. The winds have increased to twelve miles per hour and are expected to rise to fifteen. There's a front headed this way."

David frowned. "What do you mean headed this way?"

"Two pressure systems collided and changed the rotation, and now the stronger front is moving toward the south and bringing southerly winds with it." The captain knew as well as he did the changing winds and high speeds were the kiss of death when it came to a controlled burn.

It looked like Ashley was going to get her wish after all.

"You heard Captain James, guys. Weather conditions have changed, and I've got no choice but to shut this burn down. We need to start getting water on those backfires to extinguish them."

Murmurs of agreement piped across the airwaves as the firefighters all checked in, acknowledging the change in plans.

David moved off to the left, trying to get a good look at the area and assess how things stood as the men started to extinguish the fire. A huge gust of wind blew across the open field, fanning the flames in the southeast corner. The smoke made it difficult to see what was happening, and David moved in the general direction determined to check it out.

"Captain Beckett, sparks from the fire just flew right over the burn line with that last gust of wind, and they're igniting all over the place," one of the men hollered into the headset.

"All hands to the burn line. Let's get on this and shut it down. Fast," David urged. A wildfire was the worst thing that could happen, and David prayed they'd get it under control.

"Ten-four, Chief Beckett." Captain James moved men into place from his side of the fire, and David listened to get a better feel for what was happening.

David started shoveling, trying to make the burn line wider as a precaution. Sweat poured down his face as the smoke grew thicker, the heat from the fire blowing in his direction.

"Chief Beckett, it's moving faster. You need to get out of there. Stat," Captain James directed.

"We've got to get this under control before the winds turn this into a wildfire." David coughed, the smoke making it harder to breathe. He couldn't let anything go wrong—not on his watch.

If it hadn't been for Ashley and the delay, they wouldn't be in this position. He took a deep breath, trying to think. David knew he couldn't blame her. Ashley may have changed the dates, but she certainly didn't have control over Mother Nature. Another truth—he'd never stopped caring for her and the growing attraction between them had been reignited and was just as dangerous as the fire he faced now.

Another gust of wind fanned the flames in front of him. Split seconds counted and now wasn't the time to be thinking about Ashley. David looked around to assess the situation, not liking what he saw. The smoke was now so thick he couldn't see twenty feet in front of him. A wall of flames stood between him and the rest of the team. David stepped back and spun around in search of his exit.

"I've got zero visibility through the smoke and I'm not sure which way is out. Can someone get some water and try to get me a clear path of sight?" David asked, not letting his concern show in his voice. Firefighters always needed to maintain level-headed control.

"Ten-four, Chief Beckett. We're on it," Captain James responded. The sound of voices, even if only in the headset, was reassuring help wasn't far away.

David pulled out the extra fire blanket and pulled it over his head as a precaution. He sucked in several deep breaths, choking on the smoky air as it filled his lungs. An image of his father trapped in a burning house flashed before his eyes, reminding him of what was at stake. His mother had barely survived his father dying. He didn't want to think of the agony he'd put her through if anything happened to him.

*Lord, please give me the strength and courage to face this situation in a manner that honors my father's legacy and help guide me out safely. I pray you'll take care of my mother and Ashley if this doesn't end well.*

David moved off in the direction he felt was correct, trusting and hoping that his team would get to him in time because, without a doubt, he was in trouble.

# Chapter Sixteen

♥

THE SOUND OF VOICES came racing across the wind, and Ashley stopped to figure out what she was hearing. "Trent, listen."

"I hear it. That's an awful lot of shouting. I wonder what's going on?" Trent frowned. "We need to get out of here."

"I totally agree. Although the voices are getting closer, so I'm pretty sure we're about to find out what's happening, whether we want to or not." Ashley watched as several firefighters came charging toward them.

"Trent? What are you two doing out here? This area is closed. You need to get out of here. Stat," one of the firefighters ordered.

"Sorry, I didn't see the sign, Captain James." Trent shot her a dirty look. "What's going on?"

"Fire department business. Scott, can you escort them back to their vehicle and see that they leave the area," Captain James ordered, the urgency in his voice unmistakable.

Ashley dug in her heels, not willing to leave until she knew what was happening. David was out there, and with the smoke blowing this way, her worry button was short-circuiting. "We know there's a controlled burn going on. And Trent and I are friends of David Beckett. Surely you can tell us something."

He nodded, a grim look on his face. "I know exactly who you are. Ashley Stanton. The woman who decided the picket line and media show was a good thing for the fire department to wake up to this morning." Captain James' opinion of her couldn't be clearer. "Trent, you need to get your sister out of here."

"I'll do that." Trent nodded. "But the only way I'm going to get her to budge is if you tell us what's going on. Please. I know my sister all too well." Good for Trent, standing up to the man. It was his best friend out there and he wanted answers just as much as she did.

The two firefighters looked back and forth between each other. "Get going, Scott. The others are already arriving, and I'll be right behind you after I take care of these two." The man ran ahead into the woods, and Captain James turned back to them. "The winds changed speed and direction. The fire line circled back, and one of our firefighters is currently trapped. We are trying to get to him through this side. Now leave, please." Several other firefighters came running in their direction, Kojak leading the way.

"Which firefighter?" Ashley demanded.

"Chief Beckett." Three words that had the power to gut Ashley, her heart lodging somewhere in the vicinity of her throat.

"Come on, Ashley. We need to get out of here and let them do their job. For David's sake." Trent pulled her by the arm, urging her to go.

Ashley went with him, but she wasn't leaving. Not the way they thought she would. The parking lot would be a safe place to watch, but she wasn't going farther than that. She jerked her arm out of his hand, turning back to watch Kojak and the men disappear. She closed her eyes, hoping to fight back the sudden rush of tears.

Trent pulled her in his arms. "He'll be okay, Ashley. It's David. He's one of the toughest guys I know, and he'll be fine. And Kojak's one of the best fire dogs I've ever seen. He won't let anything happen to David."

Ashley raised her head and frowned, trying to pull herself together to be strong. "And exactly how many fire dogs have you seen in your life?"

"One." He frowned. "Come on, I promised Captain James we'd leave." Ashley gave in, and the two of them trekked back to the parking lot in silence.

David's life was far more important than the eagle, and it took this moment for her to put things into perspective and to realize what she'd done and the repercussions. It was her fault the burn had been pushed back a few days. Which made it her fault David was in danger. The idea of losing him was more than she could bear.

Ashley was still in love with David, while he, on the other hand, was still *out* of love with her. Nope. Things hadn't changed—not one bit.

She touched the eagle pendant safely tucked under her shirt.

*Please, Lord, keep him safe. Please don't take him from me. Not this way.*

David froze, glancing in every direction, unsure of where to go next. Adrenaline raced through him as his flight or fight reactions warred with one another. The problem was, he didn't know where to fly or how to fight back.

Sweat stung his eyes, blinding him. He tried to push away the thoughts of his father, but he couldn't. Had his father known what was happening? David sucked in a deep breath, wondering if it would be his last.

He moved a few steps backward. Or at least what he thought was backward. He wasn't going to give up hope. His team was out searching for a way to get to him. He trusted them.

The flames became more evident through the smoke, which meant he was moving in the wrong direction. He turned to the right and then to the left, trying to decide which way to go. While he still had a breath left in him, he wouldn't stop believing his team would get to him in time. The heat was suffocating. He felt like a dancing chicken on a hot plate as he tried to find his through the maze of flames to escape.

And then he heard it. A distinct sound different from the crackling fire raging in front of him.

*Woof. Woof. Woof.*

Kojak was close. David closed his eyes, searching out the sound and the direction it was coming from. *Come on, Kojak, bark again.*

*Woof. Woof. Woof.*

David turned to the left and started forward, slowly at first, and then breaking into a run as Kojak's bark got louder. Seconds later, Kojak grabbed his arm and pulled him forward.

"Boy, am I glad to see you, buddy." David couldn't control the rush of emotions surging through him as he brushed back the tears from his eyes. He trusted his fire dog with his life, and with Kojak by his side, he knew everything would be okay. The smoke started to grow less dense, and within seconds, Kojak barked one last time. Suddenly, there were firefighters everywhere, rushing to get to him.

"Chief Beckett, are you okay?" Captain James asked. "Thank God, Kojak found you."

David coughed. "I've had better days. But a little fresh air, and I'll be all right." He nodded.

"We've got him, and he looks pretty good, all things considered," the Captain alerted the rest of the team using his headset. Loud clapping could be heard all the way back from the South Summit entrance.

"Marty and Scott, help him out of here. I'll notify the paramedics you're on your way. I've got to stay here with the others and make sure we get this fire put out."

"Ten-four, Captain James." Two men supported him, one on each side. For a guy who always liked to be in charge and do things on his own, he was grateful for their support. Kojak ran ahead. The dog had earned himself a huge steak dinner, a whole lot of love, and a medal of honor.

"Good job, Kojak," he called out to his faithful friend. The dog stopped to look back at him. It was almost as if he nodded before turning back to lead them down the trail.

A couple of paramedics met them as they drew closer to the parking lot. The winds had shifted, moving the fire line in this direction. Unfortunately, it had crossed into the territory Ashley had been trying to protect.

They came to the South Summit parking lot, and the place was full of vehicles, including an ambulance. Not that he needed one as far as he was concerned. But he also knew protocol. The paramedics would make sure to give him a thorough once-over, and then he'd have to be cleared by the doctors before he could return to work.

As they drew near, David spotted Ashley. She was the last person he wanted to see here. David frowned, noticing her tear-streaked ashen face, the image hauntingly familiar. It reminded him of his mother the day his father died. Ashley had no business here, and he wanted her gone.

She came running in his direction when she spotted him, Trent not far behind. He'd have a few things to say to him about this later when they were alone. His friend should have had more sense than to let Ashley be anywhere near here.

"Are you okay?" she asked, her lower lip trembling. This was an Ashley he'd never seen before, and he hoped he never would again. Not even when they broke up in high school had she seemed this devastated, wearing her emotions for all to see.

David tried to pull himself together.

"Is he okay?" she asked the men when he didn't answer.

"Yes, ma'am. He'll be fine. But we need you to step aside so we can get him medical treatment." A fresh wave of tears rolled down her cheeks.

David pulled the oxygen mask from his face. He was emotionally and physically drained, but there was one thing left he needed to do before he gave himself over to medical care completely. "Ashley, I'll be fine. You have no reason to be here. Go home."

She winced, not taking his rebuke well.

He knew she was here because she cared about him, which made it harder to push her away. But he couldn't let it stop him from doing what needed to be done. "The reason I told you not to be here is that it's dangerous. You see what can happen even to someone in the fire department who knows what they are doing. What if it had been you out there? Is everything you're doing worth leaving Cory motherless?"

Ashley reeled back as if she'd been slapped. "How dare you?"

Trent took a step forward, his jaw clenched—the warning duly noted.

The comment was harsh, but he'd said it because of his own fear. After facing his own mortality, David thought the remark more than justified. And her anger was far better than her tears.

Today had proved with a certainty, there could never be anything between them. It was better this way, even if it meant ripping his own heart out in the process. "Trent. Get. Her. Out. Of. Here. Now." David turned away, allowing the paramedics to help him into the ambulance. Anything to get the look on Ashley's face out of his head.

# Chapter Seventeen

A SHLEY STOOD FROZEN IN place, wholehearted-
ly stunned and completely devastated as she
watched the group of men help David into the ambulance. A sick feeling pooled in her stomach. A
fresh wave of tears fell down her face, but she didn't
care.

Trent wrapped his arm around her shoulder.
"Come on, Ashley. David means well. He's been
through a lot, and we need to give him some breathing room."

"Breathing room? I think he wanted more than
that from me." A sense of déjà vu washed over her.
When would she learn? David would always break
her heart.

"Perhaps it's for the best," Trent said, his voice
low but filled with meaning.

Not that it mattered, but she wanted the truth. "What's that supposed to mean? What is it you still haven't told me? I deserve to know the big secret; don't you think?" Ashley refused to get in the car until her brother started talking.

"I don't really think it's my place to tell you. It's just something David shared once when we'd had a little too much to drink one night while we were in college." Trent shook his head, holding out his hand for the keys. He was in full-blown protective mode and not about to let her drive. Even if it was her car.

Ashley knew she wasn't capable of the focus needed and wouldn't argue the point. She wouldn't put anyone in jeopardy willingly, contrary to what David thought. She loved her son too much for that.

"Tell me, Trent. I think I have a right to know. I care about David, and you know it. But right now, I'm hurting. The man I love, have always loved, just tore me to pieces with his words. I need you to help me understand why." Ashley handed Trent the keys and then wrapped her arms around her midsection, staving off the cold chill seeping through every pore of her body. She slid in the passenger seat, fighting the urge to let loose another torrential downpour of tears.

"Ashley, I'm sorry. I know how much you care about him. Have always cared about him. Right now, he's upset and not thinking clearly. Give him time to recover. David was basically just pulled out of the fire and saved from a horrific death. If you really care, cut him some slack." Trent let out a deep sigh. He started the car, putting it in reverse to back out of the parking space.

It was right for them to leave. It was a place Ashley never wanted to see again. "Tell me what you know," Ashley asked, speaking softly, hoping to break through Trent's armor.

"Fine. I've already told you I ordered David to leave you alone and I've explained why."

"Well, he didn't exactly fight for me, did he?" She shook her head. The truth still had the power to hurt.

"No. But David had his reasons. In a way, I think he got in over his head with you, and I gave him a way out. For what it's worth, I believe David cares for you. A lot. The problem is, David saw his father die in that horrible house fire, watched it all unfold on TV. And ever since then, he's watched his mother suffer. She's been living in a shell of grief, and nothing David's done has helped her. His mother refuses to join the real world. David has had to protect her and take care of her and watch her suffer through her unhappiness.

"He was driven to follow in his father's footsteps to honor him and what they'd once dreamed of sharing. Working together, side by side. Father and son. But in choosing the fire department, he was equally choosing to never have a relationship so that he never hurt someone as much as his mother was hurt."

Ashley closed her eyes, taking a deep breath. She'd always known losing his dad had been tough on David, but she'd never realized it was this far out of control. Her heart ached for the young boy who had watched his father die and then was forced to become a man and take care of his mother.

She'd been right all along. David wasn't just sending her away from the fire, he was sending her out of his life. *Again.* "Thank you for telling me."

Trent reached over and squeezed her hand. "I know you've had a rough couple of years, Ashley, but it'll get better. You're strong and always manage to come out of it."

"Thank you. I don't quite see it that way at the moment but give me time. This has been a lot to deal with in one day."

"I'll take you home. We can leave my car at the scenic vista and come back for it tomorrow. Okay?"

Ashley nodded, happy to let someone else take control. At least for the moment. "We need to pick up Cory from Tricia's place." Right now, she wanted to hold her son more than anything, needing the emotional connection. For a little boy, he packed a whole heap of love.

"No problem," Trent said.

They drove back in silence, Ashley exhausted and heartbroken.

Several days passed, and Ashley hadn't heard a word from David. Trent assured her he was doing well, but although she watched for him, he seemed to come and go at odd hours as if to avoid her.

The rest of the burn had been postponed, which should have made her happy, but instead, she couldn't shake the guilt for her part in disrupting the fire department's original plans. It had taken a couple of those days for her to gather the courage to return to the South Summit area but resuming her search for the eagle was still important. She sucked up her courage and tackled her fears head-on. It gave her something to do to keep her mind off David, wondering if he was truly okay. Not that she expected to spot the eagle—certain the fire and thick smoke would have driven him away if he had existed.

Seeing the burned area forced her to relive the moments of fear when she'd thought she'd lost David. And spending hours at a time alone in the woods did nothing to calm her nerves or her memory. The only thing that helped take her mind off the situation was when she and Trent finished the booths together for the festival. David was taking time off from work to recover, but it also meant he was staying away from his festival obligations. Or more than likely—her.

Trent was quick to say his absence had nothing to do with her. But Ashley wasn't sixteen anymore and wouldn't buy into her brother's attempts to make her feel better. Not like she used to.

*David blames me.*

Ashley checked her emails, her gaze immediately going to the one from National Geographic. She clicked on the email, holding her breath, knowing this could be exactly what she needed in her life.

*Dear Ashley Stanton,*

*We reviewed many applications for the position of executive creative photographer. Several candidates came highly qualified, including you. We are pleased to inform you that you are the one we'd like to offer the position to. The level of artistic creativity in your photographs is beyond compare. Your attention to detail is fantastic, and we appreciate that you can see beauty beyond the obvious interest one might see at first glance.*

*We would love to welcome you to our team. Please let us know if you'd like to accept this position so we can move forward with the processing. We would require you to work out of our headquarters in Washington D.C. Your first trip would be to South America two weeks after you start.*

*We hope to hear good news from you. Again, congratulations.*

*Sincerely,*

*John Bellevue, CEO*

She'd gotten the job.

Ashley couldn't believe it. Tears rolled down her face, something that happened all too easily these days. At least this time, it was something good that made it happen.

*Her dream job was hers for the taking.* And other than having to make it work traveling with Cory, nothing was holding her back. David's recent rejection had forced her to face the truth about the two of them and her feelings.

*Unrequited love.* The perfect definition of their relationship, or lack thereof.

She would probably always want him, but she didn't need him. Instead, she needed to rely on herself and to make the best decisions for her and Cory. This job was the sign she'd been waiting for. Confirmation it was time to move on to new beginnings.

Ashley didn't need days or even hours to figure out the answer. She immediately hit the reply button and typed out her response.

*Dear John Bellevue,*

*Thank you so much for your beautiful words and the amazing offer. I would love to accept the job. There are a couple of things I must attend to here in Hallbrook before I can leave, but I expect to arrive in Washington D.C. in about a week. That should give me plenty of time to find a place to live and report to work as per your letter.*

*Again, thank you very much. I look forward to working with the entire National Geographic team. This is such an honor.*

*Ashley Stanton*

*P.S. South America sounds exciting. Can't wait.*

"What you reading, Mommy?" Cory asked, coming to stand next to her.

"Mommy just got a job offer. Isn't that exciting?" Ashley smiled, wanting to share the joy with her son and anyone else who would listen.

"Yay, Mommy. You're the best picture taker ever." Cory threw his arms around her neck and hugged her.

"We're moving to Washington D.C. in a week. That's our country's capital. Doesn't that sound great?" His inquisitive nature would love all the wonderful things offered. It was a kid's dream place to live, the activities endless.

Cory frowned. "You mean we can't live in Hallbrook?"

"No, darling. The job is in D.C. You'll love the National Zoo, the Air and Space Museum, the Smithsonian museum, and tons of other places."

"But it won't have Uncle Trent. Or Mr. David. Or Kojak. They're my friends. Just like Chloe and Bryan are my friends. If I'm in a new place, I won't be able to play with them." His eyes filled with tears.

"That's part of moving, honey. You make new friends. You're good at that." Ashley tried to encourage him. Cory's reaction was not what she'd expected, and it was enough to toss a bucket of water on her earlier joy.

"But I like the ones I have," Cory mumbled, his lower lip trembling.

"It'll be all right, I promise." Ashley's heart was breaking for her son, but change was a part of moving on and starting over. They'd have each other, and that's what was most important.

Ashley needed to call Trent and Tricia to share the great news. Hopefully, someone would be happy for her. This was her dream, after all.

# Chapter Eighteen

♥

DAVID WAS TREATED AND released from the hospital with orders from Chief Anderson to take some time off. The first three days were mandatory to allow him time to get over the smoke inhalation, and he didn't argue about it.

The following seven days were a long overdue vacation. The burn was now out of the question and would be for several months to come. The summer wasn't typically conducive to the right conditions. It could be fall before everything could possibly line up again. Hopefully, campers, hikers, and day guests would be extra careful. Just in case, however, David vowed to stick around the area to be on hand to help if any fires did break out.

Driving to Lancaster to visit his mother gave him time to think about Ashley. He knew he'd hurt her, lashing out the way he did. And if he hadn't known, Trent made sure to remind him of it each time they spoke. Seeing her tear-streaked face and knowing the danger he'd faced had crippled him. His love for her had forced him to react, sending her away from the area and from him. It was the only way he knew to make sure it worked.

And now, he was prepared to live through those moments again because his mother would want every detail. Not that she'd get what she wanted, but he'd tell her a modified version before she had a chance to hear it from someone else. David pulled up in front of the medical facility, finding a parking spot close to the entrance. He headed inside, making his way to the front desk. "Good morning, Angie," he said, shooting the older woman a friendly smile to match her own welcoming one.

"Good morning, David. Here to see your mother?" Angie had a knack for remembering the families of patients as they came and went, personalizing the experience and putting people at ease.

"Yes. Do you know where she's at?" he asked.

"Let me check." Angie picked up the phone and called to someone beyond the double doors that led to the patient care area. Seconds later, she looked back up at him. "She's in her room. I know she'll be thrilled to see you. It's a Wednesday, so this middle-of-the-week visit will be quite a nice surprise for her." The receptionist was one of those people who saw everything as sunshine and roses and was perfect for dealing with patients' and their families.

"Yes, it will be." David nodded. "I took some time off from work and wanted to squeeze in some extra visits. Hopefully, it won't be long before she is able to come home."

"She's doing quite well, so maybe only another few weeks. She's definitely perked up lately," Angie added, an extra twinkle in her eye.

"Oh? Anything special happening?" he asked, his curiosity piqued.

Angie winked, her grin widening. "Nothing I'll be talking about."

"That good, huh? Guess I'll have to get it straight from the source." He chuckled, walking away in the direction of the door.

"You do that," she answered, pressing the button to release the lock on the doors.

David made his way to his mom's room, stopping only long enough to knock before walking in. "Hope you don't mind a visitor," David called out.

"David! What are you doing here? Not that I mind, but this is unexpected. What a great surprise." His mother's face was lit with love and joy and a smile from ear to ear. It was a genuine smile, one he hadn't seen the likes of in a very long time. She was...glowing.

"Glad I could put a smile on your face." He leaned down and kissed her on the cheek. "Although, from what I hear, it might not be because of me. Rumor has it you've been smiling a lot lately. What's going on?" He was thrilled, of course. For years, he'd tried to bring light back into her life and failed, which made him even more curious about the change.

"You should know better than to listen to the rumor mill. You'd think you get enough of that in Hallbrook."

There was no way he was letting her off the hook without telling him what was going on. "Then tell me the story, so I get it straight from the horse's mouth." He chuckled.

"Last time I checked in a mirror, I wasn't a horse. As for a story, there isn't one. I'm just happy. Can't a person be happy without a story?" She looked out the window, avoiding his gaze.

"I haven't seen you this happy since... In a long time." He'd almost brought up the unmentionable and could have kicked himself in the backside for doing it. But oddly enough, her sunny expression didn't falter.

"I'd rather hear what brought you my way. Aren't you supposed to be working?" She fixed her gaze back on him, laying her hand across his.

"Fine. Didn't figure you'd hold out on your own son. As for me, because I *don't* keep secrets from my mother—" he grinned, unable to keep from teasing her, "—I thought I should tell you what happened a couple of days ago before you got wind of it and started worrying about me. Figure if you hear the story from this horse's mouth, you'll handle it better."

"Now you're a horse? What is it with you and horses? Clearly, I can see you're okay. You are okay, right?" Her brow deepened into grooves as she gave him the once over, top to bottom, as if to ascertain his well-being for herself.

"I am." He nodded.

She pulled him closer. "Tell me what happened."

"We were doing a controlled burn out near the North Summit area. Circumstances put us behind schedule, and it ended up being a bad day. The winds picked up and changed direction. It was a little harrowing for a while, but everything's fine." He intentionally left out his involvement and near disaster.

Her eyes darkened and there was no evidence of her earlier relaxed demeanor. He expected nothing less and sought to reassure his mother. "There's nothing to worry about." David patted her hand.

"Why are you not working today?" she asked.

David knew full well she was flashing back to the past, something he preferred not to be the cause of, but it couldn't be helped. It had been a tough choice between shielding his mother from more pain and honoring his father. And as it turned out, there was nothing he could have done to change his mother's reaction to what happened. That was something only she could do for herself.

"Because the fire chief wanted me to take a couple of days off to rest." He wouldn't lie to her, only evade full disclosure. "But I've also decided to take the week off and use up some vacation time."

Her eyes narrowed; disbelief etched in her expression. "Vacation? You never take vacation time. What's going on, David? And don't sugarcoat it. I'm your mother, and I have a right to know." He hated it when she pulled out the motherly tone, the one she used when she wanted answers.

"Nothing's going on. It's no big deal. I inhaled some of the smoke, and time off is a precaution only. The vacation time was my own idea, I promise. I'm thinking about long walks in the woods with Kojak and taking time to appreciate God's wonderful beauty that's all around me, but that I never stop to enjoy." It was the truth. Mostly.

"Sounds to me like you're a bit shaken up by your experience. Call it mother's intuition."

"Ashley's back in town." A change in subject would be good, and Ashley's name was a surefire way to do it. His mother had always loved Ashley and never understood why he'd ditched her. She'd never let him forget he'd walked away from a per-

fect young woman who loved him, not that he needed reminding. It was something he lived with every
day all on his own.

"That's wonderful. How's she doing? Have you
finally come to your senses and told her how you feel
about her?" His mother pressed for the details, but
she wouldn't like the answer any more now than she
had when he was eighteen.

"She's good. Her son looks just like her. Ashley's
leaving town as soon as she finds a job, so don't go
getting any ideas." He and Ashley weren't capable
of being *just* friends, no matter what they said to
the contrary. And all he'd managed to do was put
hope back in both their hearts.

"When you see her, be sure to tell her she better
not leave without stopping in to see me." His mother
was letting the matter drop, another surprise, but
one he was okay with.

"I will. She's living in your place for the time
being."

"Oh? That's news. What's going on?" his mother
asked, her interest zapping back to full strength.

"Nothing. There was a house fire where she was renting, and she needed a place to stay. No big deal since you're not ready to go home yet."

"I see," his mother said, her grin widening.

There was nothing to see, but his mother wasn't about to believe him. "Do you want to go for a walk, or would you rather play a game of checkers?"

"We can go for a walk. The doctor keeps encouraging me to do it more and more, so this should make him happy." His mother's sunny mood had returned.

"A walk it is. Do you still need the walker?"

"Yes. But the doctor thinks I should be able to graduate to the cane next week, and if I do good, I can go home. If I don't have any falls, that is. He's very protective, just like you." She patted the back of his hand.

"That's awesome news. I'm going to put in a lift for you to get up to the apartment. There's no way you can handle those steps when you come home. Far too dangerous."

"I wouldn't go to all that expense right away," his mother said, her voice hesitant. She headed out the door, leading the way down the hall.

Something was definitely up. "What's going on, Mother? Why shouldn't I put the lift in?"

She let out a deep breath, stopping to look up at him. "I wasn't ready to have this discussion with you, but it seems I have no choice. I've had a lot of time to think, and I want to get a place of my own." His mother started down the hall again as if she hadn't just dropped a verbal bomb.

"A place of your own? You already have one." She wasn't making any sense. David held the door open for her as they headed outside.

She shook her head and smiled. "I mean a place of my own where I'm not living next to my son and having him underfoot all the time because he feels the need to baby me. I appreciate everything you've done, but I'm ready to take back control of my life. Something I think is long overdue." His mother was talking crazy.

"I don't baby you. I'm protective, caring, and helpful. In other words, a good son." He frowned.

"Babying," she said, her matter-of-fact voice hitting home.

*His mother was serious.*

"What's wrong with what I've been doing?"

She let out a deep breath before continuing. "It's come to my attention that perhaps your protectiveness is enabling me to not move forward with my life." His mother turned to look at the gardens as they passed, avoiding his gaze once again.

"Explain." He'd listen to what she had to say. And then veto it.

"I know this is a difficult subject for you, but now is probably a good time to have it. Ever since your father died, I've been a basket case." She held up her hand to stop him from interrupting. "I know I've gone through periods of anxiety and depression and craziness, and you stepped in to fill your father's shoes, for which I shall be forever grateful. While I've been rehabbing here, I've also been seeing a therapist. I'm getting counseling that's long overdue."

"Counseling is good." He nodded.

"It has been. I never really got over your father, which is why I could never rejoin the real world." Tears filled her eyes, and David's heart ached for her, but she wasn't telling him anything he didn't already know.

He wanted her happiness more than anything, and though he might not like the changes she was proposing, he had to admit she looked better than she had in a long time. *Happier.* "And now?"

His mother grabbed a tissue from her pocket and dabbed at her cheeks. "And now, I feel as though I have closure."

"Let's sit for a while." David stopped at one of the benches and helped his mother down onto the bench, and then sat next to her. "What do you mean?" he asked, knowing the discussion was long overdue.

"Your father loved me, and he showed me his love in everything he did and in everything he said. I realize now how unhappy it would have made him to see me still grieving after all these years. He knows how much I loved him. Your father would have wanted me to embrace life with the love and laughter I shared with him. By not being that person anymore, I've lost what he loved most about me." His mother placed her hand on his arm, urging him to understand.

David leaned over and hugged her, trying to give her emotional support. "Those are some pretty deep revelations, but I admit, they make sense. Is this what prompted you to think about getting your own place?"

She pulled back and looked him square in the face. "I know this is going to come as a shock to you, and unfortunately, there's no other way to tell you but straight out. My doctor and I have been spending some time together when he's not at work. I enjoy his company. He comes by, and we play games, talk, and watch TV. We laugh and have fun together."

"Aren't there rules against that?" David asked, his face drawing into a scowl. The idea of the doctor taking advantage of his mother was one he wouldn't tolerate. No matter what his mother said to the contrary.

"Stop it. It's not like that. It hasn't been like that. And it won't be for two more weeks until I'm discharged." Her tone was challenging. *Motherly.*

"What's that supposed to mean? What happens in two weeks?"

"This is exactly why I need my own place. I'm your mother. I can make my own decisions and don't have to answer to you. When I get out of here, the doctor and I are going to take our relationship to the next level. We're going to date." She grinned, as if the very idea brought her happiness.

David didn't see it the same way. "Mother, you can't be serious?"

"Oh, but I am. I've realized through grief counseling that I've hung on too tight. I wouldn't trade the years I had with your father for anything, not even the painful ones after the accident. It was better to have him for the time God allowed us together than not have him at all. But now it's past time for me to let go and move on. And luckily, I found someone I want to be friends with when I leave here. I don't know what'll happen with it after that, maybe nothing. But I've agreed to give it a shot."

David was in shock. His mother sounded stronger and better than she had in years. And he couldn't deny it was a good thing. How could he fault the doctor for encouraging his mother how to live again? Especially since they hadn't crossed the lines of professionalism. As much as David hated to admit it, his esteem for the man rose higher instead of lower. "Can I ask you something?"

"Of course," she answered, a questioning look on her face.

"You say you wouldn't trade those years for anything. Even now, knowing the horrible outcome. But I remember the grief and how long you couldn't function. How can that be fair to you?" David's voice was raw with emotion, or at least it sounded that way to him. It reflected the pain in his heart. Everything she'd said today was a complete contradiction to what he believed. To the way he carried out his life.

"Your father loved the fire department. It was a part of who he was. I understood the dangers and accepted those when I agreed to marry him. There are lots of jobs that don't have risks, or ones not nearly as dangerous as firefighters face, but then people die every day going to and from work. Accidents happen.

"What happened to your father was an on-the-job freak accident. Horrific, but not an everyday occurrence in the fire department. David, any woman you ask to marry you that says yes, will be strong enough to handle anything life throws her way. I know you, and I know the type of woman you would care about. She won't be a simpering mouse, but instead, a strong independent woman."

David let out a deep breath, the thoughts in his head spinning like a merry-go-round. Everything he'd believed since his father died twelve years ago no longer made sense. His mother was saying her grief was her own fault for letting it take control of her life. Did she really not regret marrying his father in the first place?

What did that say about Ashley? She was strong and independent, just like his mother said. The idea of putting her through something so traumatic was like a knife to the heart. But then so was the sting of the knife from walking away from her.

He'd already lost almost eleven years he could've had with her. Eleven years that he'd spent as a firefighter and he hadn't died. Eleven years they could've been married and had a family.

*Cory could've been his son.* He shook his head, his eyes watering.

"Are you asking for any particular reason?" His mother's voice was gentle and soothing, bringing him back from the destructive thoughts.

"I told you Ashley's back in town. But according to Trent, she got a job offer from the National Geographic, and she's leaving in a week." She'd worked hard for that job and deserved it. He would never stand in her way of achieving her dream.

"You let her go once, which I never understood. Based on the questions you're asking me now; I think I understand a whole lot better. And I'm sorry. I feel like I've misguided you through some of the most important years of your life. I didn't realize how much I was affecting other people. Mainly you.

"David, you can't let her go again, not without telling her what's in your heart. I can tell you still love her. Your voice changes each time you say her name, much the same way your father's voice changed when he said mine."

His mother was right, he did love her. Had always loved her. And now, David didn't want to let her go, but therein lay the problem. He'd hurt her far too often to expect her to forgive him or to ask her to stay.

*'If you love something, set it free. If it comes back to you, it's yours. If not, it never was.'* The

famous quote by a man named Bach described precisely how he felt in this moment.

"I've said some things recently that I can't take back. Things designed to drive her away. I never wanted to see her go through what you did. Does that make any sense?"

"Of course, it does, David. But it's even more the reason you can't let her leave without telling her how you feel. You have to try." His mother's words of wisdom might have worked before he'd run his mouth this past Sunday.

"She'll never listen to me." David shook his head. He'd had two chances and managed to mess up both.

His mother smiled. "Then go one better. Show Ashley. Actions speak louder than words."

David thought about it as they resumed their walk through the gardens. *Show her.* Maybe his mother was right.

The easiest way to show Ashley was to prove he believed in her. She believed the eagle existed, and although David helped her search once and moved the lines, he hadn't really supported and encouraged her, truly believing in her cause. In other words, he'd been more patronizing than supportive.

David knew the mountain just about as good as anyone and had been the perfect person to help her. He should have been out there with her every day, instead he'd let her do the searching on her own. "Thanks, Mom. I think you're right. And I have just the plan. Say your prayers, and let's hope Ashley's been right all along about the eagle. If he's around, I'm going to find him. Before she leaves."

His mother grinned. "Wonderful." She stopped to kiss his cheek. "Now, go claim your sweetheart."

David spent the rest of the morning with his mother, catching up before heading back to Hallbrook. The ride gave him the time needed to work out the details for a plan of attack.

The first person on his list to call was Trent. It was time the two of them had a heart-to-heart. He dialed his friend's number and was relieved when he answered. "Hey, it's David. Got a few minutes to talk?"

"I'd say so." Trent's voice was crisp with tension, a clear signal he still hadn't forgiven David for hurting Ashley the way he had. Not that he blamed

Trent. He'd be pretty upset if the situation were reversed. But David hoped that their history and friendship would buy him some wiggle room.

"Let's cut to the chase. I know I was out of line with Ashley the other day. But you and I both know you didn't want me dating her in the first place, and I didn't want to date anyone. I didn't plan for her and me to reconnect while she was in town. I was just as determined to put an end to it as I was before—for all the same reasons." They'd never discussed the past, and it was time to clear the air.

"But you handled it with concrete gloves. That's my sister you hurt, and I've got a problem with that. The first time, I understood and let it happen because I believed it was for the best. This time, there's no excuse."

He needed Trent's help if this was going to work, and that meant putting the issues aside. "I agree. But for now, can we table the rest of the discussion and move forward. I don't have much time," David asked, hoping their friendship would count for something. There were a few seconds of silence, but he waited, letting Trent make his own decision.

"Fine. What's going on? Have you recovered from the smoke inhalation?" Trent asked, his words a good indication he'd accepted the truce.

"Thanks for asking, and, yes. I'm taking some time off. I went to see my mother today. She told me a few things, and we had an eye-opening conversation. I don't intend to get into it with you now. I'd like to talk to Ashley about it first."

"Good luck with that. I'm not sure Ashley's willing to talk to you. And I already told you she's leaving soon."

"That's why I need your help. I want to give her a reason to talk to me. A way to show her how I feel about her. But I need your help." David couldn't help but glance up at the skyline in search of the eagle Ashley believed existed.

"What makes you think the third time will be a charm?" Trent asked, disbelief evident in his voice. "What's changed?"

"I don't know how it will end up, but I know I need to try. And my mother pointed out to me that actions speak louder than words. I want to show Ashley that I've had a change of heart about a lot of things."

"So, you're not planning on hurting her again?" Trent was still in big-brother-protector mode, but David didn't mind. Not one bit.

"No. I'm planning on marrying her if she'll have me." It was true. He'd wasted almost eleven years, and he didn't intend to wait another day. That is, if he could convince Ashley to trust her heart.

"Wow. Didn't see that coming. That must've been one heck of a conversation with your mother." Trent's voice had relaxed and become more friendly.

"It was. Will you help?" David asked.

"We've always been best friends, but I've been told in no uncertain terms to butt out of her life and that I've interfered enough. You've got your work cut out for you my friend."

"Ashley knows?" David's stomach felt like it had dropped a hundred feet off a cliff.

"She dragged it out of me and isn't happy with either one of us."

"Great," David said, his level of hope slipping a notch or two. Convincing Ashley would be even harder than he'd expected.

"What do you need from me?"

"Ashley's got a map with all her grids marked out that she's been using for the eagle search. I need you to snap a picture of it without her knowing. I need to see what territory she's covered and what's still needs to be searched."

"She's not doing the search anymore. She sent a letter to the Audubon Society with a report of all that's occurred and let them know she's leaving town on Sunday for the new job."

David still couldn't believe she would just pick up and move on. "She might not be searching for the eagle anymore, but I am. And I'm hoping it'll be more than just me out there." David needed a whole lot of luck, community help, and answered prayers.

"Count me in, for sure. Ashley had her heart set on finding that eagle and truly believed he was out there, but now, she's pretty sure the smoke would have run him off."

David also worried about that, but he had to search. Otherwise, none of them would ever know the truth and he didn't want it to come between him and Ashley. Ever. "We won't know for sure either way if he's already gone, but if the eagle is still here, we need to find him. And that means searching the rest of her territories and rechecking the others. A complete search."

"I'll head to her place now and see if I can get a picture of it, or better yet, I'll snag the map, since she won't be using it anymore," Trent said.

"Stop in at my place, I should be home in about fifteen minutes. I want to make plans for tomorrow. Right now, I need to make a few more phone calls. I want to show Ashley a little community love, Hallbrook style. But more specifically, my love." He would pull out all the stops to make this work, for Ashley and their future.

"I'm on it," Trent said before disconnecting the call.

David was grateful for his friend's help, now, he all he had left was prayers. To find the eagle and win over Ashley's forgiveness and her heart.

# Chapter Nineteen

♥

RIGHT AT SEVEN A.M., David pulled into the South Summit entrance. He was pleased to see several cars already there, one of them Trent's. Armed with a dozen cups of coffee and just as many donuts, he wanted to give everyone a warm welcome. It was his way of saying thanks to those who'd managed to fit this into their schedule at the last minute.

"What kind of luck did you have rounding up people?" Trent asked him as he approached.

"Six confirmed plus us. It's a workday, so I'm pretty happy we were able round up a few. Most of these guys need to get to back to work after lunch so we need to step up the plan and do double coverage on the areas search. What's Ashley doing? Any chance she'll show up out here?"

"No. Tricia's guests left this morning, and the girls are headed to Lancaster for a relaxing day out while Harry watches the kids. Ashley wanted to do something nice for Tricia for all the childcare she's done for her this past week. It's a girl thing. Glad I wasn't invited." Trent scrunched up his face in distaste.

"Sounds like something good to miss." David chuckled.

"Where's Kojak?" Trent asked, looking back at the truck.

"It was easier to leave him home this time, what with trying to coordinate people and the search." Kojak had pouted and retreated to his bed when David told him he couldn't come this morning. It had almost been enough for David to change his mind. Almost, but not quite.

"I bet he hated being left behind."

"Oh, he did. But I promised him a nice long walk later today to make it up." Not that the promise did anything for a sulking dog.

"What's today's agenda?" Trent asked as the others who had already arrived formed a circle around them, waiting for instructions.

The group was a little on the sleepy side of seven, and David handed out the coffee and pastries. "We head out at seven-fifteen. Here are the eight gridded areas Ashley hasn't checked yet. These are the four we will cover today. I'm assigning two people to an area since we have limited time today.  I've got a copy of the mapped out sections for each one of you." David reached in his pocket for the maps, giving them to Trent to hand out.

"You need to check treetops, keep an eye on the skyline, and keep your ears open. I've got compasses for everyone to mark the points you cover in the box." He pointed to the carton on the ground he'd set there when they first arrived. "The compasses were left over from the kid's outdoor nature course we taught at the fire department last summer. Nothing fancy, but they'll do the trick." David glanced around the group to see if there were any questions.

"What about the extra areas?" one of the guys asked.

"With today's turnout we'll cover most of what we need. Unfortunately, I've got an appointment and can't stay out here this afternoon either. I'll pull a double tomorrow and finish up on Saturday." It was the best he could do and the only way to cover all the sections before Ashley left on Sunday. David hoped his efforts would be enough to convince her of his feelings and his dedication to her cause. And his belief in her.

"I don't mind helping. I figure I owe you one." Trent grinned.

"Glad you think so. But if you keep disappearing right before she's due to leave, she's liable to get suspicious. Maybe you can keep me posted about what she's up to. And don't let her leave town early. Maybe you could even sweet talk her into staying till Monday."

Trent nodded. "I'll see what I can do. Ashley's hunches have always been pretty good, and as long as the smoke didn't run the eagle off, I'm betting on her gut instinct."

David sucked in a deep breath as the group all murmured in agreement. His friend's reminder about the burn and the smoke caught him off guard, and images of being trapped in the fire assailed him. He hadn't given any thought to returning to the place where it happened.

"David?" Trent caught him by the arm. "Are you all right?"

David forced his attention back to his friend. "I'm fine." Or he would be once the images stopped flashing in his head. He took a deep breath and exhaled. Pulling the list out of his shirt pocket, he read off the pairings and called out their sections. The sooner they moved into action, the sooner it would quell the sick feeling in his stomach. Or he hoped. "Don't forget, pictures are critical for proof. Even if it's just a suspected flyby, take the picture, and we can check later to verify or rule out."

The group divided and started off, everyone in high spirits, hoping to bring this eagle watch to a successful conclusion, and thereby putting Hallbrook on the map.

David and his partner, Brandon, one of the local law enforcement officers, searched high and low. The next few hours had resulted in many bird and wildlife sightings, but there was no sign of the eagle. They were all due to meet back up at the parking lot soon and none of the teams had called in a sighting—the silence of his phone like a death knoll to his high hopes.

Once their allocated time was up, the group met back in the parking lot to compare notes. They dispersed after David reminded them to keep the search efforts quiet from Ashley. The last thing he wanted to do was get her hopes up for nothing. He'd done that enough on his own.

"Trent, make sure you keep me posted what she's doing tomorrow, especially if she manages to ditch you again and show up out here." David grinned.

"Will do. And David, let's let the past go, okay? I know I shouldn't have come between the two of you, and I'm sorry. But we're adults now and I'd be proud to have you as my brother. Just thought you should know that."

"Sounds good to me. But it's not as if your permission will do me any good now."

"I know walking away the first time couldn't have been easy, but if you walk away this time, it won't be on my hands. My advice—fight for her. She's worth it."

David nodded and let out a deep breath. He was glad the two of them had settled their issues. Now, he just needed to fix things with Ashley. "You're right, it wasn't easy to walk away because I love your sister. Always have and always will. You have my word. And I won't be walking away. This time it will be up to her."

Trent leaned in and gave him one of those grizzly bear man hugs that only two close friends could share. "Good to hear. You have my vote."

Ashley had fun today hanging with Tricia. A relaxing day out had been exactly what she needed. And knowing she had a new job just around the corner had eased her normally tight budget spending limits enough for her to treat Tricia. It was the perfect way to thank her friend for Cory every day while she'd gone traipsing through the woods in search of the eagle.

The only problem had been that whenever she thought about the eagle, she thought about the fact she should be out there searching. The idea of unfinished business was driving her crazy. Ashley didn't have to leave until Sunday, which still left her all day Friday and Saturday.

Once she made the decision to head back into the woods, she felt better about everything. Besides, it would be a good chance for Uncle Trent to have some quality time with his nephew before they moved. Her brother didn't know it yet, but he'd be flying solo tomorrow. He'd find out soon enough tomorrow, because telling him ahead of time would give him more time to try and talk her out of it.

Ashley poured a glass of iced tea and sat at the kitchen table. Cory was playing in the living room, giving her a chance to check her emails after being gone all day. Pulling out her phone, she checked her account, knowing the HR department from the National Geographic had mentioned they'd be sending her a contract of employment for her digitally sign and return.

Mostly junk mail, she skimmed through the subject lines, deleting as she went. Ashley stopped on one, the subject and sender catching her attention. La Galleria had finally responded to her inquiry about a showing. She'd all but written them off due to a lack of response. Her heart raced as she opened the email.

*Dear Ashley Stanton,*
*We appreciate you reaching out to us regard-*
*ing a showing and apologize for our response*

*time. The committee was very interested in your portfolio.*

Ashley stopped reading, disappointment washing over her. 'Was interested' said it all. Not that it would have mattered now anyway. She was headed for D.C. to be a part of the National Geographic team. But still, it would have been amazing to have her own show.

She was about to hit the trash button when a few of the words down the page caught her attention. *...offer you a permanent showing...*

Wait. What? Scrolling back to the top she started to read the letter again wondering what she'd missed.

*Dear Ashley Stanton,*

*We appreciate you reaching out to us regarding a showing and apologize for our response time. The committee was very interested in your portfolio. La Galleria is dedicated to presenting our clients with quality works of art and usually bring in collections on a limited basis. However, after much deliberation by the committee it was decided that your collection would be best presented in an alternative fashion.*

*We would like to offer you a permanent show-ing location within La Galleria. As your work sells, you would be expected to continue adding other pieces of artwork at the same high quality and caliber as those already in the collection. Please let us know if you'd like to join the us in Boston at La Galleria.*

*Sincerely,*

*Tom Duncan*

*La Galleria Managing Director*

Ashley shook her head, the words sending her into a spiral. A joyous, mind-numbing, completely insane spiral. Two dream jobs in the space of a week. She jumped to her feet and spun around in a happy dance.

"What's a matter, Mommy?" Cory asked, watching her as though she'd gone bananas. Which, of course, she had.

"Mommy got another job offer and she's just excited." Ashley picked Cory up and spun him around.

"Does that mean we get to live here now?" Cory asked, a light in his eyes.

Unfortunately for his sake, it didn't mean that at all. "We still need to move. Both jobs are in different places, but now we have a choice. Trust me, honey, Mommy will pick the best one for both of us."

The light in his eyes faded just as quickly as it had appeared. His response took away from some of the joy of the moment, but it wasn't anything less than she'd expected. To a four-year-old, moving was moving.

"Can I watch Disney?" Cory asked, turning away.

For him, the conversation was over. For her, the conversation in her head was just beginning because now, she had the problem of deciding which job to take.

# Chapter Twenty

♥

B Y MORNING, ASHLEY STILL didn't have an answer. She taped up two more boxes and put them in the living room. The amount of stuff she had leaving town wouldn't come close to filling a U-Haul truck like the one she'd driven across the country to Hallbrook. Now, everything she owned would fit in her car.

From the moment she'd received the email from La Galleria, her world had shifted into a state of inner turmoil. The biggest factor she had to consider in the decision was Cory because what was best for him, was ultimately what was best for them both.

Over the past week, nothing she'd said or done seemed to get her son on board with leaving. It didn't help they hadn't seen David or Kojak, but perhaps it was for the best. The excitement she'd thought she'd feel from taking on a new job still hadn't settled in. Of course, now, the added issue of not knowing which job, wasn't helping. Neither did the sadness of leaving Trent and Hallbrook again. And David, if she was honest.

Once she decided, Ashley would make it work. There was no doubt that the minute she was back in action taking pictures, she'd be in her element and at peace with the world. And either job she took would allow her to do that.

The people at National Geographic were expecting her soon, but she wasn't worried about them filling the position if she decided not to go through with the job. There would be hundreds of photographers lined up to take her place. Except it was her dream job and she'd be a fool not to take it.

But then, having her own gallery showing had also been a dream. And this one was even better than anything she'd dared hope for—a permanent showing. Two offers, both wonderful, made the decision next to impossible. But it was one she needed to make. Soon.

"Cory, honey, we've got to run an errand this morning before we head to Uncle Trent's. Can you put on your shoes, please?"

"Okay, Mommy." Cory retrieved his shoes from the front door and sat down on the couch to put them on. His energy level was next to zero. He wasn't one of those kids that acted out when he was unhappy. He just kept things bottled up inside. *Like David.*

It had come as a shock when Trent told her the truth about David's past. The problems he faced ran deep, making him emotionally unavailable. It was like a huge red no-go zone hanging over his head.

Ashley poured herself another cup of coffee and sat at the table, going through her backpack while she waited for Cory. Most of the time, he managed to put his shoes on himself, especially with the Velcro sneakers he'd chosen to wear. As she pulled everything out one by one and went over her mental checklist, she realized she was missing the most important thing...her map.

Ashley frowned, digging deeper in the bag and checking all the zippered pockets, sure it was still in there. She checked around the house, but the map was no wear to be found.

"I'm ready, Mommy. Look, I did my own sneakers." Cory smiled, proud of his accomplishment.

"Great job, honey. Guess we're ready to go." Hopefully Trent would have one she could borrow. If not, she'd have to go on memory alone, because no matter what, she was going today.

After stopping at the store for more snacks to take with her today, Ashley drove to Trent's place. Cory unbuckled himself from his seat and pushed open the car door. He jumped out and raced to the front porch, pressing the buzzer multiple times.

"Just once is all you need, Cory," Ashley said, relieved her son was excited about something. And that something was his Uncle Trent.

The door opened and Trent stepped out on the porch to join them. "Hey, kiddo." He lifted Cory up and tickled his belly. "Are we going to have a great day, or what?"

"The bestus, Uncle Trent." Cory beamed.

"Morning, sis. Come on in. I'll be ready in a few minutes."

"Good morning. Um, I have a favor to ask. Why don't you make today a Cory and Uncle Trent day? Just the two of you," she emphasized.

"Why? Where are you going?" Trent frowned.

"I want to go look for the eagle." She crossed her arms and steeled herself for his response.

"Ashley, enough is enough. Family time is important too. I haven't seen much of you at all and now you're blowing out of town again. I'd like to spend the day with my sister."

"What about me, Uncle Trent?" Cory asked.

"Of course, you. Always you, buddy." Trent chucked Cory under the chin.

"Maybe we can do something tomorrow. I'm not leaving until Sunday morning," Ashley tried to appease Trent. She would have liked to spend more time with him also. Building festival booths together hadn't exactly been what she called quality time.

"Fine. But I'm going to hold you to it. You're going to miss all the fun I had planned, but that's more fun for me and Cory to share." Trent said, tickling Cory again. Her son was eating up the attention.

"I'm sorry. Truly. Oh, and do you have a map of the park? Mine seems to missing, although I swear I left it in the backpack."

Trent frowned, shaking his head. "I don't. Maybe it's one of your signs you're not supposed to go back out there."

"Maybe, but I don't always follow the signs. Clearly." Ashley grinned, remembering when she'd driven around the roadblock.

"Trust me, I know." Trent rolled his eyes as if the words weren't enough.

"I'm going to the lower southeast quadrant and I basically remember the section, so, no worries. I'll figure it out." It wasn't her normal organized way of doing things, but sometimes, you had to make do. And this was one of those times.

"Call me if you need anything."

Ashley kissed Cory and waved goodbye to her two favorite guys. "Be good for Uncle Trent, Cory," she called out as she walked away, eager to start her last search for the bald eagle. Maybe today would be her lucky day.

David headed out early, relieved when he hadn't run into Ashley. He drove straight to the South Summit parking lot and headed back into the woods, Kojak by his side. They made good time in the cold, crisp air, trying to stay warm.

He'd only been out in the woods for about twenty minutes when his phone rang. "David Beckett."

"Hey, it's Trent. Thought you should know that Ashley is planning on searching for the eagle today. She just came by and mentioned the missing map, but I did find out she's planning on searching the lower southeast quadrant. Not sure which one you're in, but you might want to stay out of there unless you want to run into her."

It was one of the areas he planned to search tomorrow if nothing turned up today. That would be one less gridded section for him to check, and it meant they would have all been covered by the time Ashley left town. "I wonder what changed her mind?"

"Her determination and unwillingness to accept defeat, I reckon." All things David loved about her. "Thanks for the heads-up. Where's Cory?"

"Uncle Trent's on duty today. We were all supposed to hang out together, but the eagle won out over her brother by the looks of it." Trent laughed.

"Sounds like fun. He's a great kid."

"I couldn't agree more. Which is why Ashley needs to stay in Hallbrook. Cory needs a male influence in his life and someone to play ball with. Someone like you and me. Any progress on your end?"

"No. But I'm working on it, trust me. Later." David hung up and intensified his search. He brought his lunch and only stopped for a few minutes here and there to look around and breathe in the fresh mountain air.

Trying to see the forested area through Ashley's eyes, he soaked in the little things. Like the fancy mushroom growing on a tree, or a strange-looking bug that appeared like a warrior in a full suit of armor and a deadly spiked back that looked ferocious.

The pictures he took wouldn't be nearly as good as anything Ashley took, but he was proud of them. Especially the one of Kojak checking out the battle-ready bug. Overly cautious but curious, the dog sniffed the bug out, getting almost eye to eye, but seeming to have enough sense not to mess with it. David agreed with Kojak's assessment—the thing had *do not touch* written all over it's scary-looking body.

It felt a little strange out here searching, all the while knowing Ashley was out in the woods doing the same thing not far from here. It was oddly comforting.

He came to a clearing that looked out over one of the larger ponds. Walking around the edge of the water, he snapped several pictures of turtles sunning themselves. He had to be quick before they plunged into the water to escape the intruders, mainly Kojak.

David sat down in the tall grass, letting the dog splash and play fetch as he threw a stick for him. It wasn't long before Kojak grew weary of the game and laid in the water to cool off.

Taking advantage of the moment, he plucked one of the tall grasses to stick in his mouth and lay back in the grass. Five minutes passed as he watched the clouds float overhead, carried across the sky by the gentle breeze. It reminded him of a game he'd once played with Ashley when they'd tried to decipher the shapes of the clouds. It had been the first time he'd held her hand, and his first awkward move to show he wanted to be more than friends.

They'd grown closer, much to the dismay of Trent. But David hadn't been in control of his heart and couldn't help falling in love with her. It was his brain that eventually rejected the idea, leading him to make what now appeared to be the biggest mistake of his life.

David sat up, catching sight of Kojak coming out of the water. The dog shook a couple of times to dry out his fur. It was time they got back to work.

A large black bird caught his attention off in the distance. He watched, unable to stop the sudden rush of adrenaline. Wishful thinking and hope would do that to a person. More than likely, it was just another turkey vulture. He tried to remember what Ashley said about the V, the W, and the straight line. This appeared to be more of a straight line, but he couldn't be sure. The bird flew closer, and David lay back down in the grass, calling Kojak to his side. "Lie down, boy." The dog lay down next to him, his head cocked to one side, questioning David's odd request.

The bird circled again, this time drawing nearer, close enough for David to see a patch of solid white, which ruled out the vulture. An osprey also had some white coloring, so he tried not to let his imagination run away. An unverified sighting accomplished nothing.

A loud screeching cry split across the sky. And then another as the bird continued to circle. David tensed; almost positive it was the eagle, the solid white of the bird's head becoming more visible.

Slowly, he lifted his phone and switched it to camera mode. "Stay, Kojak." He needed to make sure the dog didn't give away their location. Not that the osprey or eagle couldn't see them—their eyesight some of the best in the animal kingdom. But if they weren't moving, they'd be less of a threat.

David snapped off a few pictures, even though the bird was still a great distance away. Suddenly, another bird came flying out of the treetops and began soaring toward the first one. They flew together as though they were dancing and playing together in their own private world.

Whether osprey or eagle, he couldn't be sure, but it was a remarkable moment. Soulmates that mated for life. Anything could happen to either one of them, but it wasn't keeping them from enjoying today and this very moment. Another reminder of his mother's words. He just wished it hadn't taken this long to understand the truth.

One of the birds came closer, plunging into the pond and capturing a fish in its talons.

This close, the identity of the bird was no longer in question. The white head and solid brown body clearly marked them as bald eagles. The bird flew off to the nearest treetop, most likely to eat their fresh fish dinner.

Spotting the eagle was fantastic, spotting the pair was a gift from God. Shivers of excitement raced through him, the joy of his discovery only just now beginning to set in.

*Ashley had been right.*

David was relieved the smoke hadn't driven them away, but more than likely, judging on his location, he had Ashley's change of perimeter line to thank for that. He jotted down his coordinates, not wanting to lose track of the exact spot. Where there was a pair, there was sure to be a nest. And the eagles wouldn't go far from it, especially not this time of year if they had a successful mating season.

He couldn't wait to share the discovery with Ashley. David pulled out his phone to call her. It rang several times before David hung up, not wanting to leave her a voicemail. Either she didn't have her phone on, or she wasn't taking his calls. He just wished he knew which one. "Come on, Kojak. We need to get back and see if Ashley's car is still here." The dog seemed to understand as the two of them raced back, following the trail that would take him to the parking lot the quickest. Because what he wanted most was to bring her to this exact spot, tell her how he felt, and to ask her for another chance. His third and final one, because it was the only last chance he'd need.

Unfortunately, when they arrived it was only to find Ashley had already left. Poor timing at it's best. It would be too late to come back out tonight.

# Chapter Twenty-One

♥

*NOCK. KNOCK.* ASHLEY HADN'T been expecting Trent this early. She pulled open the door, surprised to see David standing there instead. She tensed, unsure of what to say or how to act.

"What can I do for you?" Hurt shadowed any attempt to be nice, Ashley stepping forward as she tried to keep Cory from seeing who was at the door. Her son hadn't stopped asking about David and Kojak.

"Good morning, Ashley. I know I wasn't very nice the other day, and I wanted to apologize." David looked good standing there, except his confident smile was nowhere to be found.

She didn't want to think about it. Or David, for that matter. She needed him gone. "Great. Consider yourself forgiven. You have nothing to feel guilty about now."

David let out a deep breath. "I'm not apologizing out of guilt. I'm doing it because I want to and because it's coming from my heart. I was wrong and I'd like a chance to explain why I was such an idiot."

"I don't need to understand anything." She started to close the door, except David moved his foot against it, preventing her from closing it all the way.

"Ashley, I know this is asking a lot of you, and you have every reason to say no, but I'm hoping you'll say yes. I need you to come with me so I can show you something." David's gaze never left her face, as though he was willing her to say yes.

Curiosity killed the cat—but Ashley wasn't a cat. There was no harm in asking, or at least the way she saw it, there wasn't. "This thing you want to show me, do you have it here? Because I'm not going anywhere with you." She folded her arms across her chest, like a shield for her heart.

"I do and don't." He grimaced. "Please, I need you to trust me at least one more time before you write me off." His voice was low and pleading, touching a soft place in her. The same place that always wanted to believe the best in him. Her heart.

"Why should I trust you? Give me one good reason."

"Because you know deep down that I care about you. Because you know you've always meant a lot to me, and that you still do."

Ashley sucked in a deep breath. He'd said the words almost as if they were a vow. She'd be a fool to believe him. "You have a miserable way of showing that." Ashley shook her head in disbelief, but her heart soared. Apparently, it hadn't gotten the message yet.

"I agree. And honestly, that's what I want a chance to talk to you about. But first, I have a surprise." David smiled, and that's all it took for Ashley to break. One smile. *Drat the man.*

"I'm supposed to be meeting Trent at the park for a family day before I leave tomorrow." It was her only defense and a weak one at that.

"Postpone it until later. Please. Call him and tell him I'm taking you somewhere—I'm sure he'll understand."

"Mr. David. Mr. David, you came back. Did you bring Kojak? Are we going somewhere?" Cory's face was lit with excitement as he hugged David's leg.

David knelt to hug her son, his gaze landing on Ashley. The genuine affection she saw on his face only reinforced her decision to hear him out.

"Yes, Mr. David has come to take us somewhere special. We can meet up with Uncle Trent later this afternoon. I see you already have your shoes on. Great job, Cory." Ashley shot a quick glance at David, catching the sudden look of relief on his face.

"I'm a big boy now, Mommy. Big boys always put on their own shoes. I'm ready to go. Where are we going, Mr. David?" Cory's non-stop chatter eased the awkwardness in the room.

"You'll see. It's an adventure walk, something I know from experience you really like. And yes, Kojak is in the truck waiting for us." David grinned, picking up her son before he stepped out onto the landing. He glanced back at her. "You coming?" He wasn't wasting any time. Probably afraid she'd change her mind. "Oh, and bring your camera. I'm not sure, but you may need it." His cryptic comment left her baffled, but definitely curious.

"Sure thing." Ashley grabbed her camera bag and headed out the door, following them down the stairs. "I heard you've been out of work for a couple of days because of the smoke and I saw your truck in the South Summit parking lot yesterday." It had been weird when she realized David wasn't far away while she searched, but she'd pushed it out of her head, not wanting to dwell on the information.

"Is everything okay at the burn site?" She'd wanted to call and ask him herself but couldn't bring herself to do it. Giving him the satisfaction of knowing she cared was the last thing she'd wanted to do after his harsh dismissal.

"Yes. And taking the first three days off is a mandatory precaution for the department. I'm actually on vacation now." He shot her a smile before setting Cory down.

"I didn't know workaholics took vacations."

"They probably don't." He laughed. "But I would like to think I'm trying to undo my workaholic status." He grabbed Cory's car seat and moved it to the back seat of his truck. After everyone was buckled in, he backed out of the driveway and headed north.

Cory talked non-stop to them and to Kojak, making it difficult for regular conversation, which was fine with Ashley. It also gave her the time to fire off a text to Trent, putting him off until later this afternoon. David was right, he hadn't minded. Which considering the fuss he made yesterday about her not spending enough time with him, made his easy dismissal odd.

They passed through the White Mountain National Forest Park entrance and soon made a turn down an all-too-familiar road. "Why does it look like we're heading to the South Summit parking lot?"

He glanced her way. "Because we are."

Ashley winced. "Back to a scene I'd rather forget. You can turn around right now," she insisted. "I don't want to see anything at the burn site."

David shook his head. "Trust me on this." His smile led her to believe this wasn't a bad thing.

*Bring your camera.* Ashley glanced down at the camera bag clutched in her hands. Adrenaline shot through her with lightning speed. There was only one thing that would surprise her out here that could be good. But it was impossible. Or was it?

Ashley reached out to grab David's arm, every muscle in her body tense with anticipation. "Tell me it's true. Does this mean—"

"It does," he said, turning into the parking lot. David shot her a wide boyish grin, one that reminded her of the way he looked after the first time he'd gotten brave enough to kiss her.

"I don't understand. Are you really telling me you saw the eagle?" She wanted there to be no mistake in what he was telling her. This was too big.

"No. I didn't see him," David said, a glimmer of mischief in his eyes as he delivered the bad news. "I saw them."

Ashley's mouth dropped open. She was at a loss for words. Tears filled her eyes, and she brushed them away, her thoughts racing out of control at what all this could mean. For starters, if it was true, there was no way she could leave tomorrow. Even if she opted to take the National Geographic job, she'd need more time to finish out documenting the eagle pairing and to find the nest. There was no way she'd leave before it was done or before she had the photographs she would want for her own collection.

"Who did you see, Mr. David?" Cory asked. "Are there people living in the woods?"

David smiled at the innocent question. "I'm sure there are people in the woods, but hopefully not living there, at least, not in these woods. But I saw the eagles your mommy has been looking for."

Ashley didn't know how or why David had done it, but the joy in her heart was overflowing. "Tell me everything. Where were they? Was there an immature? Did you see a nest?" She fired off the questions, not giving him a chance to answer.

David chuckled. "No to the immature and nest. But I've marked the coordinates on your map as to the where. I'm taking you there now, hoping we can see them again."

Ashley frowned. "My map? How did you get that? I wondered where it disappeared to."

"Trent had a hand in that." David grinned as he swung Cory up, putting him on his shoulders.

"Trent?"

"Yes. Your brother and about half a dozen people in the community came out Thursday and helped search for the eagle. We searched four more of the sections, but unfortunately, came up empty-handed. And I heard you were searching this one," he said, pointing to the one she'd searched yesterday.

"Let me guess, Trent told you? He did a good job acting clueless when I asked him about the missing map...the stinker."

David nodded. "Of course. I was over here, checking out these two areas. This is where I spotted the eagles." He pointed to a spot on the map. "There's a pond here, one with fish. Good-size fish judging by the one the eagle caught yesterday. I know we may or may not see them today, but I wanted to bring you here personally so that you'd know where to come and watch."

"And you know for a fact they're eagles? Do you have any proof? Not that I don't trust what you saw, but anyone I tell will want proof. Especially if I try to get federally protected status for the area."

David smiled and set Cory down. "I have pictures. Relax. They're not great, but I'm guessing you can mostly confirm what I know I saw with my own eyes."

"Show me," she urged, unable to contain her excitement.

David pulled out his phone and flipped through his gallery of pictures. He turned it around for her to see when he found one he liked.

Even through her tears, Ashley could tell he was right. It was a bald eagle. "Oh, my goodness. It's a miracle." She flipped through the other pictures, stopping at the photo that captured both eagles in one shot. Not an easy feat.

"It is at that. Follow me." David took Cory by the hand, and the three of them headed toward the designated spot, Kojak leading the way.

"I don't understand why you were out here doing this," Ashley said, following him through down the trail.

"Someone recently told me actions speak louder than words. I wanted to show you how much I care. About you, and everything you believe in. I can see my mother was right. I told you at your house that I cared about you, and your face darkened in disbelief. Now, I'm showing you, and you're listening. I know this is important to you, and I wanted you to see it through to the end before you leave for D.C."

"You did this for me?" Ashley asked in wonder. He was still David, the man she loved, but a different David. A better David. One that would be even harder to leave behind.

"Of course. I've regretted some of my decisions in the past a hundred times over, none more so than walking away from you.  You see, I had this thing about not wanting you to have to deal with tragedy if something were to happen to me in the line of duty. Like my mom."

"Trent told me as much recently." The question was, could she trust in the words? Too often, she'd trusted men, and her judgment had failed her.

David glanced back at her and let out a deep sigh. "So maybe you can begin to understand at least a little. It wasn't until recently that I talked to my mom about it, and by way of a miracle, she's moving on with her life and stepping out of her grief. She made me realize that even had she known how things would end between her and my dad, she wouldn't have changed loving him or marrying him. That just blew my mind and gave me a lot to think about."

"That's what real love looks like. It's the dance between two people for as long as God gives them."

"That's what I've come to realize." David grabbed her hand and pulled her into the clearing. "This is where I spotted the eagles. I don't see them right now, but I was lying here yesterday afternoon, quietly praying for another chance with you when they appeared. I took it as a sign. I have a picnic lunch so we can sit back and relax, and maybe, just maybe, we'll get to share the magical moment together."

They all moved to stand at the water's edge, Cory checking out a frog and completely ignoring them.

"I still can't believe you did this. Do you realize there must be a nest near here?" Ashley asked, gazing around.

"That's what I thought. We'll just have to keep looking until we find it."

"Sounds like a plan to me." She smiled. David moved closer, his gaze landing on her mouth.

Ashley knew what was coming, and she welcomed it with all the love and joy in her heart. David had shown her how much he loved her. And the much-awaited kiss would confirm it.

"Look, Mommy. There's a big birdie in the sky over there." Her son interrupted the kiss, but neither of them could stop from looking at where Cory pointed.

David focused the binoculars he carried. "Good eyes, buddy. Good eyes." He looked over at her and nodded.

"Really? It's the eagle?" Ashley asked, pulling out the zoom lens for her camera. There was no way she would miss this. She screwed it in place and adjusted a few settings based on the lighting.

"It is. Yesterday, I had to wait until the eagle was a lot closer because I left the binoculars in the car. Here, take a look." David handed her the field glasses.

She let the camera hang from her neck, dying to get a glimpse. As she watched, a second eagle joined the first, and they soared gracefully together. "They're beautiful," she whispered. I can't believe it."

"Believe it. Now, you need a good picture. Something better than what I took." He grinned.

Ashley pulled the compact tripod from her bag, set it up, and attached the camera, while David went to work and laid out the blanket. He and Cory sat down to watch the eagles, the two of them eating snacks while she tried to get the perfect shot. Kojak lay close by waiting for Cory to drop, or sneak, him some food.

She adjusted the focus, trying to bring the birds into view, and zooming in for better details. The birds flew in circles, and it was difficult to keep up with them with any degree of clarity. The tripod action just wasn't fluid enough to move in multiple directions with of efficiency.

"I'm just not getting anything," she said, frustration edging into her voice. It was a momentous occasion, and she needed to document the sighting. "I've got an idea. Sometimes it's a little easier to move the camera on something that gives me more room to operate and adjust, but something that's still somewhat stationary."

"You lost me." He laughed.

"I need you. Stand up, and I'll use your shoulder as a prop for the camera. I can move it around faster because it's not actually attached to anything."

David nodded and stood. "Okay, then. Use me. I like the sound of that." He chuckled.

"As a tripod." She grinned.

"Disappointing."

Ashley moved to stand close to David, one hand on his shoulder as she steadied the camera. "Hold still. They're coming back around. Do you see them, Cory?" Ashley asked.

"I do, Mommy. Those are big birds. Way bigger than the ones in the backyard."

"Yes." She laughed. "Way bigger."

Ashley clicked the shutter button repeatedly as the eagles drew closer. She followed one, and then the other, watching in awe at the majestic picture they painted. Suddenly, one of them disappeared into the woods. The other one circled back around, before it, too, vanished into the woods.

"Give me your binoculars, David. I bet the nest is somewhere close to where they just flew into the forest." Ashley was beyond excited at this point. The nest had to be there; she just knew it.

David came to stand next to her, handing her the binoculars.

She searched the trees, back and forth along the treetops. Eagles like the tallest trees in the area, preferring pines and upper branches. But with all the leaves on the trees, it was difficult to see any-thing. The nest was well-hidden if it was there. Not to mention, her focus was slightly off having him stand so close. Couple-like close.

"I see it. I see it," Ashley exclaimed, trying to keep her voice under control so as not to have it carry on the wind and scare the eagles. I can't tell if there are any eaglets in it, but it's huge and right near where the pair flew into the woods. Here, your turn." Ashley handed him back the binoculars, wanting to share the moment with David. After all, the discovery was largely due to his efforts.

"I don't see it, sorry. The trees all look the same to me. A lot of greenery." David smiled, lowering the binoculars and returning to the blanket where Cory and Kojak sat side by side.

"Let me check." Ashley sat down next to them and started flipping the button to go through her playback mode, zooming in on a couple of the pic-tures that appeared promising. "I've got one. See." She held out the camera to show David the shot. There would be no doubt in anyone's mind they'd found the bald eagle based on the picture. Correc-tion. Eagles. The photo had captured them both.

Ashley showed Cory the picture.

"Yay! I can't wait to tell my friends. We found them." Cory grinned. "Now we have to stay here, right, Mommy? These are our eagles." The hopeful expression on his face reminded her all too well of the challenges they still faced. She and David may be on the same page, but they wouldn't be living in the same place. Once again, fate was determined to separate them.

"We found the eagles, but they don't belong to us. They're wild," Ashley explained, shoving away the negative thoughts crowding into her happy place. Finding the eagles had changed her departure date but finding David—well that made her choice about which job to take easier.

The National Geographic would have been a fantastic opportunity, but Ashley was leaning toward the equally fantastic opportunity with La Galleria for two reasons. Cory needed family and that meant staying closer to Trent. The other, even more important reason, however, was that it would keep her closer to David. Her heart knew giving them both another chance was the right decision and Boston was just a heartbeat away from Hallbrook.

David pulled out his phone and pressed a few numbers. "Good evening, Chief." He glanced over at her and smiled.

"Yes, sir. Sorry to disturb you at home, but I have new information I think you need to know immediately. Ashley Stanton has discovered a pair of eagles and their nest northeast of the South Summit parking lot. I'll email you the coordinates and photos as proof. We need to cancel any future burn plans on file while Ms. Stanton contacts the Audubon Society. I'm sure they'll have this area designated as a nesting site and be granted federal protection."

David nodded. "Yes, sir. I will."

"What did he say?" Ashley asked, unable to believe how fast things would move at this point.

"He's pleased. Once he has our email, he'll take care of the rest."

"Thank you," she exclaimed, throwing herself in David's arms and hugging him, knocking him over on the blanket. His arms came around her for the first time in a long time, and the peace that came with it proved this was where she belonged.

"*Ewww*. Are you two going to kiss?" Cory asked.

Ashley turned back to her son, suddenly awkward, not wanting to send Cory the wrong message. She started to pull away, but David held her in place. Turning back, she gazed at David, ready to tell him to let her go, but the words died on her lips.

As if in slow motion, everything else ceased to exist as David pulled her head down and kissed her. The kiss was soft, slow, and sweet. His message crystal clear for her and Cory to understand.

"Does this mean you're going to be my daddy?" he asked.

"I'm working on it, Cory. I'm working on it." David laughed.

Ashley turned away, blushing under the intensity of his gaze. Her heart raced, joy filling her. A daddy meant marriage. The whole deal.

"What's this?" David reached toward her chest, his fingers closing around the pendant that had escaped from beneath her shirt. "You still have it," he said, his voice raw with emotion.

"I do. It was a way for me to keep a little piece of you with me always." Her eyes filled with tears, the revelation a deep part of her soul. It was a part that gave David the power to crush her. Apparently, she'd decided to trust him with her heart. *Again.*

David took her hand and brought it to his lips. "I'm glad. It makes this next part easier." He grinned.

"Next part?" she asked, sitting up.

"I wanted to show you how I feel. And helping you go after your dream was a way to do it. I'm sorry I was such an idiot and that it took me this long to realize I can't change what's in my heart, and the only thing I was doing was making us both miserable. That is if you feel the same way. Just to be clear this time around, I love you."

"Just to be clear, I love you, too." Tears rolled down her cheeks, the joy of finally being able to say the words again overwhelming.

"I know we have a lot to talk about, but I need you to understand something. I know your dream job is waiting for you, and that you must leave. It's important to you, so it's important to me that you take it. We can work through the long-distance thing if I know you love me. This is your time to shine, and I won't take that from you. Who knows, maybe I can move to D.C." David's eyes glimmered with tears of love, leaving her feeling like the most cherished woman in the world.

It wasn't fair to ask him to leave, even if it was only as far as Boston and not D.C. This was his home. "But you love it here. Swore you'd never leave."

"But I love you more." David leaned forward to steal another kiss.

Her heart swelled with emotion each time he repeated the words. "Actually, there are two jobs on the table. And it's only fair to tell you I haven't been as excited about the job in D.C. as I thought I would be."

"But it's your dream job. You can't give it up," David insisted. "And what's the other job you're talking about?" David's brow furrowed in confusion.

"I heard from La Galleria, a gallery in Boston. They want me to do a showing—an ongoing featured collection. It could be the beginning of a huge career in freelance work. I was leaning toward taking the gallery's offer and moving to Boston. That way, Cory would be closer to everyone here. It was my way of comprising with him since he'd vetoed moving altogether." She laughed, ruffling Cory's hair.

"I came here to start a new life, but that doesn't happen by running away. And this—you and me—makes the decision simple. I can take the job in Boston, but we don't have to leave. I can just commute and stay in the city when I need to be there. This way Cory wins—and we win."

David smiled, first at her and then at Cory, his expression full of love. "I can't tell you how glad I am to hear that. A new life with me. That sounds perfect." He pulled her close and kissed her again, sealing the deal.

# Chapter Twenty-Two

♥

DAVID SWUNG CORY ONTO his shoulders, one of the kid's favorite things. Cory had once told him it made him big and tall. That he could see everything like he was a giant. They joined hundreds of other people that had turned out for the fun, games, crafts, and great food. Tonight, the fireworks show would signal the end of the festival and the beginning of the end of the July 4th celebrations that increased the dangers to the forest. He'd breathe easier after the annual display to honor America's birthday.

Hallbrook was a town of traditions, and this one had been going on for as long as he could remember. Every year, it grew more extensive as people came from far away to join in the excitement.

"Look, Mr. David, it's a Ferris wheel. And a bouncy house. And a bouncy slide," Cory said, tapping the top of David's head. "Can we go play now? Please."

"I don't see why not. There are lots of things for us to do, buddy. Why don't we start at the slide, and I can go down with you? Your mommy can wait at the bottom to catch you."

"Are you sure you don't want me to *catch you*?" Ashley winked, her double meaning not lost on David.

"You've already caught me." He grinned, winking right back at her. David had been a fool to resist this, but he was also smart enough to realize that maybe when he was younger, he wouldn't have appreciated it as much as he did now. They'd both been through a lot to get to this point, and now, it was their season. And there was no way he would let her go. He dropped a kiss on her lips before lowering Cory to the ground. Taking him by the hand, David led Cory to the entrance of the slide and up the stairs.

"Hold my hand, Mr. David. We can do this together." Cory reached for his hand and pulled him in the direction of the slide he wanted to go down.

"Sounds like a plan, little buddy." David felt like a kid, almost as excited as Cory. They didn't have bouncy slides when he was a kid. Hand in hand, the two of them sped to the bottom. It was way more fun than a regular slide, the bouncy part easier than some of the crash landings he remembered as a child. His older body appreciated the soft landing as well.

Ashley was there to catch Cory at the bottom, making a big production of it. The little boy laughed, the sound joyful to David's ears.

"Can we go again?" Cory asked, his excitement bubbling over.

"Absolutely." David took him down the bouncy slide three more times before they moved to the next stop. The bouncy house.

"This one's got your name written all over it, Ashley."

"I see how it is. But I am younger than you, so my body can handle it better," Ashley teased, coming up on tiptoe to kiss David.

"There is that." He wasn't about to argue the truth or interfere with any excuse she came up with to kiss him.

Trent approached and stood next to David, watching Ashley and Cory play.

"Hey there, looks to me like things are going pretty good," Trent said, clapping him on the back.

"Couldn't be better." David nodded.

"I'm sorry I interfered all those years ago. Maybe if I hadn't, Ashley wouldn't have gone to California and ended up with that deadbeat ex of hers."

"Yeah, not a nice guy. But Ashley and I have talked about it. Don't beat yourself up over it. Things happen for a reason, and I wasn't ready. If I had been, I would have never let you tell me to walk away from the woman I love. I can promise you now if I didn't have your blessing, it wouldn't matter. Besides, Cory's here because of Joe, and neither one of us would change anything about that kid. Cory has been a blessing to Ashley when she needed one, and now, he'll be a blessing to both of us."

"Man, talk about a person changing as a result of events that happen in their life—practically overnight," Trent said, shaking his head.

"I was pretty hardheaded. When I was faced with my own mortality, God got my attention. But then, so did my mother." He laughed.

Ashley climbed out of the bouncy house and headed toward them. "Hey, you two, I'm worn out. Maybe it's Uncle Trent's turn to do some bouncing. This kid is like the Energizer Bunny."

"Look out, here I go." They watched as Trent squeezed himself through the opening. Uncle Trent was the biggest little kid and knew how to maximize Cory's fun, and apparently all the other kids in the bouncy house.

"I'm glad I'm not leaving Hallbrook. Cory needs family." Ashley smiled and took his hand. It was hard to believe he'd ever said no to this.

"And I need you," David said, leaning down to claim another kiss.

The day was filled with cotton candy, shooting far too many basketballs to win stuffed animals for Ashley and Cory, and enough festival food to tempt anyone into overindulging. By nightfall, he was more than ready to settle down and watch the fireworks, but not until he had a dance with Ashley. He'd been waiting all day to take her in his arms.

The crowd gathered around the hardwood plank floor set up in the center of the fairgrounds. The Down Home Country band had agreed to play, and folks wanted to dance to the hit parade of country singles the group boasted. The town had an advantage to booking the group since the lead singer was Mr. Peterson's grandson. Old man Peterson knew practically everyone in the county, his dairy farm and ice cream iconic. Not to mention the skating rink he set up every year in the winter. That was something David looked forward to doing with Ashley and Cory. But for now, he wanted to enjoy this moment.

Mayor Tucker stepped up to the microphone. "We're glad you all could make it to the 53$^{rd}$ annual Hallbrook Independence Day festival. Many thanks to all those who put in long hours volunteering time to make this happen." The crowd clapped and cheered. "The band is about ready to get started. We expect to see everyone line dancing, two-stepping, or whatever else it is you do to country music." The crowd laughed as the mayor attempted to provide some lighthearted humor.

"Before we bring them up on stage, we have another special presentation to make first. Where's Chief Beckett and Ashley Stanton?" The crowd looked around, zeroing in on the two of them and pointing.

"Right here," someone yelled.

David shot Ashley a look, wondering if she knew what was going on.

Ashley shrugged and shook her head.

"Come on up." The mayor waved them toward the stage.

"Go on," Trent said, giving Ashley a shove when she didn't move. "I've got Cory. No excuses." Trent grinned like he knew full well what was going on.

David took her hand. Neither of them liked the spotlight, but they'd get through this together.

"Hope you two are having a good night," the mayor said as they came to stand alongside him.

"We are," David answered for them both.

Mayor Tucker turned to face the crowd. "Now most of you know that a week ago, Chief Beckett and Ashley Stanton, or Anderson, as most of you think of her, discovered a pair of bald eagles and their nest practically in Hallbrook's back yard. We are pleased to take a spot on the bald eagle registry with the confirmed pair, and the government has now approved the designation status granting us full protection of the site.

"The town council held an emergency meeting, and we'd like to share the results of that discussion with you here tonight, as it's the perfect time for our announcement. Liberty and Belle are the names chosen for the pair of eagles, and they will become a part of our town's history as our new mascots."

The crowd broke into loud applause. The names were a perfect choice.

David and Ashley shook hands with the mayor. Ashley clapped with the crowd and pointed at him, trying to give him more of the credit, but David wasn't having any of that nonsense. He leaned forward and pulled her in for a kiss for all to see. They shared in everything, from the eagle search right down to the kiss.

Her flushed face was his reward for putting it all on the line. "Thank you, everyone," David said, before leading Ashley off the stage, both waving to the crowd. He wanted the band to start playing so he could have a dance with his girl.

"Thank you both," Mayor Tucker called out. "Without further ado, let's welcome Down Home Country back to Hallbrook."

Loud cheers erupted again, and everyone grabbed their partners and started dancing right where they stood. The temporary wooden dance floor was nice, but not nearly big enough. Luckily, folks knew the grass was all the dance floor you needed in the country.

David pulled Ashley into his arms. It was a moment to cherish as the stars twinkled above in the sky, and the rest of the world just faded away. It was him and his girl, just like it had been when they'd danced as kids. David would have been content if the music never stopped.

"Anyone want to go get a spot to watch the fireworks?" Trent's girlfriend, Maria, asked as they came up to stand next to them, her son in tow.

"Sounds great," Ashley said, taking Cory by the hand.

After picking out the perfect spot, they laid out a few blankets. With Cory snuggled in between them, David put his arm around the kid and around Ashley's shoulder, pulling her close.

"I love you," David mouthed the words over Cory's head.

Ashley didn't need to answer. Her smile and eyes told him everything he needed to know. She loved him, too.

Although, the words were nice also, and something he'd never tire of hearing.

# Epilogue

*E*IGHT MONTHS LATER...

Ashley glanced down at the ring on her finger, still unable to believe the changes in her life. She'd come to Hallbrook as a stopping point to starting her life over, only to find out she was home. David's proposal on the anniversary of their first date made her cry. *Still made her cry.* A lot of guys had trouble with birthdays and wedding anniversaries, so a first-date anniversary was a huge declaration of affection. *Especially given their first date was when she had been sixteen.*

Cory had flourished over the summer, and she'd watched her son go off to school after Labor Day with mixed joy and sadness. It had been a tough decision, but Cory had really matured under the watchful eye of David and Trent, and continually begged her to let him go. Of course, finding out she was pregnant not long after he started school helped make the transition easier. An Independence Day baby made perfect sense, even if they hadn't planned it that way.

Her son had been a huge help when it came to decorating his baby sister's room. David, on the other hand, was like a big baby, worried about every little thing and trying to make sure he didn't miss a single minute. Everything had to be perfect before the baby's arrival. It wouldn't be long now, and Ashley for one, was ready to welcome home her daughter.

The phone rang, and Ashley answered it right away, seeing her friend Maxine's name. "Is everything okay?" Ashley asked the same way she asked every time Maxine called.

"Absolutely. The puppies are opening their eyes and starting to move around," Maxine said, her voice filled with excitement.

Lulu and Kojak's puppies had been born two weeks ago, and it had been so hard to not let the information slip in front of Cory. "That's wonderful news. As soon as Cory gets home, we'll be right over. Don't forget our deal—we get first pick of the litter." David and Ashley had agreed it was time Cory had his own dog, not that he didn't have Kojak wrapped around his finger. But they had decided that a boy and his own dog would have a special bond, one Cory had earned.

"Of course. With eight, Cory has plenty to choose from." Maxine laughed. Have you told him?"

"No. We wanted it to be a surprise." Ashley knew that when the baby came, Cory might not be as excited once he realized how much attention it would take from him. Having a dog as his new best friend would fix the problem.

"Sounds like fun. See you soon."

Ashley called David at the fire station. "The puppies opened their eyes and are up and moving. Maxine said they're ready for people to start coming over to see them. Cory should be home in two hours, and I want to take him over there. Good lesson for what's to come." Ashley laughed.

"Okay. You can do the explaining. The birds and the bee's discussion, or in this case, the babies and puppies, are not in my repertoire."

"Chicken." Ashley loved his honesty. In fact, she loved everything about David. She was the luckiest woman having a second chance with the one and only man she would ever love.

"Yup. And proud of it."

"Can you meet me there at three-twenty?" she asked.

"Absolutely. I said I wouldn't give the talk, but hearing you tell it...I wouldn't miss this for anything." David chuckled.

"Maybe he won't ask how the puppies got here." Ashley was trying to think positively.

"Like he doesn't ask you every day how the baby's going to come out of your tummy," David said, quick to remind her of her son's overly curious mind.

Ashley waited outside Cory's classroom for him to come out. "Did you have a good day today, sweetheart?" She leaned over to kiss the top of his head.

"It was fun. I colored a picture. Look. It has you, me, my new daddy, and my baby sister. But I don't know what she looks like yet, so I had to use my magination." He held the picture up for her inspection.

"Imagination. And what a great picture. I love it. We need to put it on the refrigerator." Ashley laughed. "I have a surprise for you."

"Is the baby here?" Cory looked up at her and then back at her stomach, clearly confused.

Ashley laid her hands on her belly. "No, no yet. She's not due to arrive until closer to the July 4th festival, remember?"

"I remember. It sure is taking my sister a long time to get here." Cory shook his head. "It's a good thing I have other friends to play with until she gets here. Right?"

"We've talked about that, sweetheart. It will be a while before she's old enough to play with you, but that day will come. I promise." Ashley drove straight to their friend's house, Cory chatting away the entire time about his day at school. "I thought we should visit Maxine. We have someone we want you to meet."

"Look—" he pointed at David's truck, "—Daddy just pulled up." Ashley's heart swelled with pride every time Cory called David daddy.

Joe might have rights to the title by birth records, but the man was still clueless what it meant or the joys it could add to his otherwise selfish life. But Ashley was fine with things just as they were. David had more than earned the title of daddy.

"He sure did." Ashley smiled, helping her son out of his car seat.

"How's my little man?" David asked, scooping Cory up in his arms and tickling his belly before dropping Ashley a kiss.

"I made you a picture, but it's in the car. Do you know who we are going to meet? Mommy says it's a surprise."

David took Cory by the hand and led him inside. "I do know because it's your surprise." The two had grown close and were practically inseparable. Several months ago, Cory had mentioned he wanted to be just like his dad, a firefighter. David had taken a little warming up to the idea, but once he'd accepted it, it was full steam ahead. Even though Ashley had told him on many occasions that kids change who they want to be hundreds of times before they grew up, and that, when the time was right, Cory would know.

David took her words to heart and had made Cory an honorary firefighter. The title came complete with a special plastic red hat, fire coat, red galoshes, and of course, a badge. The picture was complete, but with one exception. Cory needed a fire dog. Something they were about to rectify. One of Kojak and Lulu's puppies would be the perfect companion for Cory.

They knocked on the door.

Maxine answered, a huge smile on her face. "Come on in. I can't wait for you to see your surprise." Maxine beamed.

"What is it, Miss Maxine?" Cory asked, still trying to drag the information out of someone.

"Follow me. Lulu wants you to see something." They moved into the living room, where Maxine had set up a quiet area in the corner for Lula, complete with blankets and cushions.

Ashley's heart melted when she spotted the tiny puppies moving around on wobbly legs, but not letting that stop them from exploring.

"What's—" Cory looked up at her, a question in his eyes. "Are those puppies? They look weird."

"Yes. They look weird because the puppies are only two weeks old," Maxine explained.

"Really?" Cory looked at David for confirmation.

"Yes, son. Really." David knelt next to Cory to watch with him.

Cory took a step closer. "I wish I could have one. That would be the coolest thing in the world."

"Well, then today must be your cool day." David grinned.

Cory's eyes grew wide as David's comment sank in. "You mean it? I can have one."

"You get the first pick of the litter since Kojak is the daddy," Ashley said, moving to stand next to Cory and taking him by the hand as they went closer.

"Wow. Kojak? That is so cool. But they all look so much alike, how will I know which one to pick? And what's wrong with them? Are they sick?" Cory's brow furrowed as he considered the puppies.

"What do you mean? They're fine, I promise," Maxine chimed in.

"But they don't have any spots. Not a one. They look like white rats," Cory said, shaking his head.

Everyone laughed. It was true, but it was unkind to voice the sentiment out loud in front of Lulu, who stayed protectively close to the new puppies. "If you look really hard, you can see the beginnings of some grayish fur. Within the next couple of weeks, all the spots will come in. It will be a surprise. You pick based on which one seems to have the personality that matches your own. The boys have blue collars, and the girls have pink. You're smart, curious, playful. So, which one do you think has the same curious playfulness? Maxine will mark it with a tag to identify the puppy as yours," Ashley said.

Cory moved closer. "Hmmm. This is a hard decision." He rubbed his chin, making a big production of the moment. "I pick...that one." He pointed to the biggest one in the litter with a blue ribbon around its neck. "'Cause he looks big and strong, just like me when I grow up."

"I think that's an excellent choice," David said. "What do you want to name him?"

"Hmmm." Cory's eyes lit up. "Smokey."

"But he'll be white with black spots? Smokey doesn't seem to fit," Ashley said, trying to figure out her son's motive for the name.

"Seriously?" David looked up at her, grinning from ear to ear. "You explain it, Cory. She needs a little help."

"Smokey, like Smokey the Bear. Only this is Smokey the dog. Both fight fires." Cory shook his head as if the answer should have been obvious. "Girls," he said, before turning back to his new puppy.

Ashley laughed. "I get it. Sorry." She held her hands up. "I don't have firefighting on the brain."

"I'll let it slide as long as you keep this firefighter on your brain," David teased, kissing her in front of everyone.

"That I can do. Now and forever."

What to read next?
Love & Honor
Book 7 of the Holidays in Hallbrook series – A Sweet Veteran's Day Romance.
Sometimes the deepest wounds can help you find the greatest joy . . .

If you enjoyed this sweet and charming romance, be sure to check out the
**ALSO BY ELSIE DAVIS** section on the next page for more clean and wholesome romance.

## BONUS READ

Want to keep in touch with new releases and what's happening in the world of Elsie Davis?
Sign up for the monthly newsletter at Elsie Davis HEA (Happily-Ever-After) and enjoy DIGGING THE DRIVER (A Celebrity Corgi Romance) as a FREE BOOK!

The greatest compliment you could give an author is to leave a review in order to help other readers discover the same great stories you enjoyed. Amazon/Bookbub/Goodreads are all great places. Many thanks!!!
Another great way to keep in touch - *Follow Elsie Davis on FaceBook*

# Also By Elsie Davis

*Sweet, Clean and Wholesome Stories...with a Happily-Ever-After Guarantee!*


***Holidays in Hallbrook***
(Sweet Romance Series for Holidays Throughout the Year)
***Welcome to Hallbrook, New Hampshire. A small-town filled with the unexpected, lots of love, and of course, a beloved dog to ramp up the excitement.***
*Love & Order (Labor Day)*
*Love & Family (Thanksgiving)*
*Love & Peace (Christmas)*
*Love & Chocolate (Valentine's Day)*
*Love & Hope (Mother's Day)*
*Love & Liberty (Independence Day)*
*Love & Honor (Veteran's Day)*

*Love & Joy (Easter)*
*Love & Adventure (Father's Day)*


**Great Smoky Mountain Getaways**
*(Christian Inspirational – Women's Fiction Ro-*
*mances)*
*Juliet's Journey to Love*
*Poppy's Path to Love*
*Rachel's Road to Love*


**Crossroads Creek Cowboys**
**(Christian Inspirational Romances)**
*The Heart of a Cowboy*
*The Help of a Cowboy*
*The Return of a Cowboy*
*Coming Soon – The Care of a Cowboy*


**Crestfield Inn Romances**
If you like special kinds of soulmates, a splash of
the supernatural, and wholesome relationships,

you'll adore this sweet bit of fun filled with romance and mystery.
*Turning Back Time*
*Turning Up Roses*
*Turning Down Pie*


**Celebrity Corgi Romance**
*(Standalone Sweet Romance)*
If you like light mystery mixed in with your happily-ever-after, you'll enjoy this second-chance romance and the race to save an adorable Corgi.
*Digging the Driver*


**Gold Coast Retrievers**
*(Sweet Romance)*
**Special Golden Retrievers help their humans solve mysteries, save lives, and even find love...**
*Defending Dakota*


**Trinity River**
*(Sweet Western Romance)*

*Ranchers and farmers depend on the Trinity River for water, but when a secret conglomerate starts buying up property by fair means or foul, it's time for the landowners of Tumble County to fight back—Texas style. But what they don't count on, is finding love in the process.*
*Back in the Rancher's Arms*
*Small Town, Big Secrets*


## Coming Soon! (2023-2024)


## Sundancer's Legacy – 9 Book series

*Sundancer's Star*
*Sundancer's Joy*
*Sundancer's Heart*
*Sundancer's Majesty*
*Sundancer's Miracle*
*Sundancer's Glory*
*Sundancer's Kiss*
*Sundancer's Moon*
*Sundancer's Splendor*

# About The Author

Elsie Davis is a *USA Today and International Bestselling Author* of over 25 sweet, clean, and wholesome romances, and a member of the ACFW. She discovered the world of Happily-Ever-After romance at the age of twelve when she began avidly reading Barbara Cartland, the Queen of Romance, and has been hooked ever since. After building her dream log home on top of a small mountain, she turned her attention to do what she loves most, writing. Elsie writes sweet Contemporary Romance and Contemporary Christian Romance from her heart...hoping to share a little love in a big world.

When she's not writing, she can be found birding, kayaking, camping, fishing, playing disc golf, and taking nature walks—hoping to spot wildlife. Basically, she loves all things outdoors, EXCEPT cold weather. She and her husband are avid Caribbean cruisers, but Elsie's favorite vacation was their cruise to Alaska. (In spite of the cold!) Indoors, she enjoys a toasty fire, and of course, a great romance with a guaranteed Happily-Ever-After.

https://www.elsiedavishea.com